Line Up for Murder

by the same author

DANGEROUS TO KNOW
THE TWELVE DEATHS OF CHRISTMAS
MURDER, MURDER, LITTLE STAR
THE LORD MAYOR OF DEATH

MARIAN BABSON

Line Up for Murder

WALKER AND COMPANY
NEW YORK

(1)

First published in the United States of America
in 1981 by the Walker Publishing Company, Inc.

ISBN: 0-8027-5453-8

Library of Congress Catalog Card Number: 81-51979

Printed in the United States of America

10 9 8 7 6 5 4 3 2 1

CHAPTER 1

On December 28 the banners went up at Bonnard's:
SALE OF THE CENTURY
BONNARD'S CENTENARY SALE
STARTS JANUARY 4

Velvet draperies had shrouded their windows since Boxing Day. Behind them, the window-dressing staff had worked furiously. Just as they disdained the brown wrapping paper with which lesser stores blocked off their windows for the occasion, so Bonnard's eschewed the racks of marked-down dresses and jumble of price-tagged goods strewn higgeldy-piggeldy across the shop-front display windows of other stores.

Bonnards always dressed their windows as carefully for their January Sale as for any of their million-pound promotions. It was not simply a matter of pride, for the Sale would bring in several million pounds' worth of business. Bonnard's took good care that it should.

This year—their Centenary Year—the January Sale was to be more sensational than ever, opening a celebratory year of Special Events, Grand Promotions and lesser sales, culminating in an Extravaganza next Christmas to wind up the year and send them triumphantly into their second century of retailing. They were starting as they meant to go on.

Since the week before Christmas advertisements had been running in leading newspapers all over the world. In Paris, Berlin, Tokyo, Abu Dhabai, New York, Chicago, Dallas, Geneva, and every wealthy city whose inhabitants, if not to be lured to that precise sale, could be reckoned upon to travel at some point in the year and would remember the advertisements and visit such an enterprising store when they reached London on their tours.

On December 29 the windows were unveiled. Mannequins in evening dress (discreetly priced at the hem) disported across a living-room as improbably elegant as a stage set when the curtain rises. (The furniture, too, was annotated by the smallest possible card at one corner, a diagonal red line through the original price and the sale price immediately below it, as a footnote.)

The reductions were so dramatic that they needed no further emphasis.

They were, of course, the loss-leaders, the crowd-pullers, the items that would be featured in every newspaper story about the Bonnard's Sale. The £8000 floor-length black mink, with cleverly concealed zipper to turn it into a hem-length coat and separate stole, on sale for £240; the £2000 imported Italian three-piece living-room suite for £150; the £1800 Persian carpet going for £75 — all were displayed in the major windows flanking the main entrance as a foretaste of the delights waiting within when the Sale started.

The queue began forming on December 30.

Dorothy Witson arrived at 10 p.m. and was distressed to find that she was not to be the first in the queue. She'd known she should have come sooner, but the others couldn't be hurried. They'd insisted on giving her a big gala dinner on the grounds that it would be a long time before she had a hot sit-down meal again. Then there'd been the fuss over the sleeping-bag and was it really warm and comfortable enough. Then the final delay because they'd wanted to wait until the very last second before filling the hot-water bottle so that it would stay hot just that little bit longer.

Really, you'd have thought she was going to the moon. At least.

Now here she was, and there were people ahead of her.

She smiled cheerfully at them, masking her disappointment. It might be all right. Time would tell.

The others were still fussing.

'Oh, Auntie Dorrie—' Young Sandra stared down at the pavement and along the bleak deserted street with an acute attack of guilt. 'Are you *sure* it's all right? You'll be comfortable enough?' She turned to her husband uncertainly. 'George—?'

'It's getting colder.' George was no comfort. 'Weather forecast said the temperature would drop tonight. We should have brought blankets—'

It was always the same. They wanted her to do it for them and then, at the last minute, they were afraid it was too much of an imposition. If they started on again about her age . . .

'Suppose it rains?' Sandra scanned the cloudy sky. 'Or snows?'

'That doesn't matter at Bonnard's, dear.' Dorrie glanced upwards complacently. The sheltering overhang protected the front pavement, there was plenty of room for people who wanted to huddle against the building. They wouldn't get wet unless there was a driving rain blown directly in upon them. But there had to be enough space for the wind to gather force before that could happen and the imposing bulk of the St Edmunds Hotel across the street provided as much protection, in its way, as the awning like projection overhead.

'Of course not.' George was beginning to assess the situation. 'Besides, there's room for her here in the entrance. The next ones along will be round the corner on the pavement. We got here just in time.'

It was true. A young couple who seemed to be newly-weds, or perhaps very early marrieds, were first in the queue, right up against the entrance doors which wouldn't be open to receive them for another five days.

Behind them lurked—it was a strange word for one

8

who was sitting peaceably in a queue, but Dorrie considered it and decided that it was not unfair; there was something about him—Behind them lurked an indeterminate man, neither young nor old, friendly nor hostile, interested nor disinterested.

Some sort of foreigner, I'll be bound, she told herself severely.

Did any of them look like the deluxe fridge-freezer?

It was hard to say.

'Do stop fussing!' She turned and surveyed George and Sandra with less fondness now. They were beginning to be in the way. She'd never find out anything with them fusspotting around.

'Yes, perhaps you're right.' George seemed to catch her mood. It was as though she were leaving on holiday, already aboard a ship but being tethered to shore by the good wishes and anxieties of those who had come to see her off. Until they left, the adventure could not begin. 'Time we were getting home.'

'It *is* getting late.' The prospect of getting rid of them restored her fondness. They were such a nice young couple. 'I'll be all right.'

'Well . . .' Still Sandra lingered. 'If you want anything, anything at all, just ring me and I'll send one of the kids down with it.'

'That's very nice of you, dear.' Dorrie emptied a carrier bag of a Karrimat, a pillow and two thick cushions and handed the empty bag to George, who took it absently. He was still looking around incredulously, as though unable to believe that anyone could be willing to put up with so much discomfort. But then, he was too young to remember the war and the nights of sleeping in Underground shelters. A few days outside Bonnard's was, comparatively (and like Bonnard's itself), the height of luxury.

The others in the queue had, naturally enough, been

stealing glances at the new arrivals, trying to work out how many of them were going to be permanent additions. The atmosphere eased as it became apparent that only Dorrie was going to become a resident member of the queue.

Dorrie crossed glances with the young couple at the head of the queue. They blinked uncertainly, then almost smiled. Not exactly welcoming, but accepting her as the newest addition to their domain. Quite right and proper. There would be plenty of time to sort themselves out and establish relationships over the next few days. The Sale didn't start until January 4.

Dorrie noted with approval that they were rather aimlessly engaged in a two-handed game of cards and that the stiff covers of board games peeped from the top of a carrier bag beside them. Monopoly, she'd be bound, *and* Scrabble. Very good games, and open to several players at once.

As she'd said before, Bonnard's drew one of the best queues in town. Such nice people—and not a bit snobbish, no matter what people thought.

'You *won't* catch cold,' Sandra pleaded tearfully. 'If you feel a chill coming on at all, just pack it in and come straight home. We won't mind, I promise you. Nothing matters except your health.'

'Yes, yes, I promise.' Dorrie patted her shoulder absently. 'I'll take care.'

'Mind that you do,' George said gruffly. 'We don't want to put your health at risk. Nothing's worth that.'

'I'll be all right.' Dorrie was hard put to keep a note of asperity out of her voice. You'd think she'd melt in the rain, the way these two carried on. Not that any rain could reach her under Bonnard's overhanging portico.

'Well . . .' Loath to leave, Sandra shivered involuntarily as she looked up and down the street again. It was bleak and desolate at this hour, with the darkest, coldest

hours of the night yet to come. Hours when the rest of
them would be in warm soft beds in the comfort of their
homes. Already the pull of her own home was strong. 'If
you're sure . . . absolutely sure . . .'

'I am,' Dorrie said firmly. 'You and George get along
now. It must be nearly time for the baby's feed.'

'Yes, it is,' Sandra admitted. 'But I hate to leave you
here alone . . . like this . . .'

'I'm not alone.' Dorrie indicated the others in the
queue. 'I'll be perfectly all right.'

The foreign gentleman immediately ahead of her in
the queue was glaring balefully at Sandra and George, as
though they were late-night revellers shouting and slam-
ming car doors and keeping him from his well-earned
slumber. Dorrie nodded apologetically to him, but he
ignored her.

'Come on.' George took Sandra's arm, evidently realizing that they would remain there indefinitely if it were
left to her. 'The baby sitter will want to be getting home
even if you don't.'

'Yes.' Sandra bobbed abruptly and pecked Dorrie on
the cheek. 'We do appreciate this,' she said. 'Really, we
do. I only wish you didn't have to stay out in the cold for
so long.'

'It's quite mild, really,' Dorrie said. 'I've been out
queuing in colder weather than this.'

'Good night—and thank you,' George said, pulling at
Sandra's arm. This time they actually left.

Dorrie watched them walk down the street and turn the
corner, waving back at her just before they disappeared
from sight. She breathed a sigh of relief and began settling
her possessions around her, marking out her own bit of
territory and making herself comfortable in it.

She spread out the Karrimat to provide an insulated
area, then unrolled the sleeping-bag on top of it, leaving
the Thermos flask in the sleeping-bag beside the hot-

water bottle until the last possible moment. Every additional bit of warmth would be welcome tonight.

The others, already settled for the night, watched her warily. Plenty of time in the morning for introductions and getting to know each other but, as a matter of etiquette, there was just one small point that ought to be settled tonight so that they could all sleep more comfortably.

'Such a nice young couple,' Dorrie said aloud, carefully not aiming her words at anyone in particular. 'I'm in the queue for them, actually. They have three small children, the youngest is only six months old, so they can't queue themselves, of course. Sandra has to take care of the children and George has to go to work —'

The foreigner immediately in front of her had closed his eyes as she started speaking, but now he opened them and half-turned on his camp bed, no longer feigning sleep but waiting. The young couple at the front were nodding encouragingly, also waiting.

'They have their hearts set on the big deluxe fridge-freezer,' she confided. 'George's uncle runs a pub and he's planning to take George into partnership with him. They want to bring along the fridge-freezer as a sort of contribution. Being so big, it will be just right when they expand the restaurant side of the pub, the way they plan to do.' Dorrie beamed at everyone impartially and waited herself.

The atmosphere had lightened perceptibly.

'We're after the living-room suite,' the girl at the head of the queue said. 'What with the mortgage payments, we'd never be able to afford it ordinarily, but I saw the advertisement in the paper and I thought, "That's it!" It's the only way we'll ever be able to get something so nice. Tim has taken the week off and we've been in the queue for twelve hours already. I was determined not to let anyone get ahead of us!'

'You'll get it, dear,' Dorrie said confidently. 'You'll be first through the doors as soon as they open.' There was no immediate competition for either of them. Unless—?

The foreigner between them stirred uncomfortably as though aware of the combined force of their expectancy. Perhaps he had been able to hold out against the implied question of the couple ahead of him but, with someone immediately behind him as well, he could no longer remain silent.

'I wait—' he said unwillingly. 'I wait for the floor-length mink coat. It is the best buy in the store.' He had grudged them the information, but it was out. He turned his head from one to the other challengingly. 'And possibly the silver fox jacket, too.'

'My goodness,' Dorrie said. 'Your wife is a lucky girl.'

'I am not married.'

'Your girl-friend, then. Is it an engagement present?'

'I am not going to marry her and not even then would I give her such an expensive present.' The man looked at Dorrie with contempt for such sentimentality. 'This is business. I shall buy the furs at this ridiculous price and then resell them for their correct value. I would be a fool not to.'

'Oh!' Over his head, Dorrie met the eyes of the young couple. It was obvious that they shared the same opinion of their queue-mate. *Nasty bit of work.* 'Well, I suppose that's your privilege.'

'That is correct.' He lay back on his camp bed, adjusted the blankets around his chin and closed his eyes with finality.

'I'm Faye Moore.' The girl spoke to Dorrie over the recumbent form between them. 'And this is my husband, Timothy.'

'I'm Dorothy Witson, but everyone calls me Dorrie—'

'Just tell me—' The foreigner had not opened his eyes, but his tone was threatening. 'Do you plan to talk all night? Have you no regard for the sleep of others?'

'Sorry, I'm sure!' *Very* nasty bit of work. And in a nice queue like Bonnard's.

The young couple pantomimed their opinion and Dorrie tried not to giggle aloud. Yes, Bonnard's was an extremely nice queue. It was just too bad that, this time, there was one rotten apple in it.

CHAPTER 2

The St Edmund's Hotel had two choices: they could en-
force the implicit understanding that only residents of the
hotel and their guests were welcome to use the con-
veniences on the lower ground floor; or they could close
their eyes to the twice-yearly genteel invasion of the
Bonnard's queue from across the street. Since the first
course might involve them in undignified scuffles along
the corridors which would disturb the regular guests more
than the thought that unauthorized persons were taking
advantage of the amenities, the St Edmund's staff and
management bit the bullet and tried to pretend that
nothing untoward was happening on those dreaded twice-
yearly occasions.

The people from Bonnard's queue, in their turn, did
their grateful best to make themselves inconspicuous
among the international dignitaries, socialites and
celebrities who patronized the St Edmund's. They might
not have succeeded entirely, especially after the queue
had been in progress for several days, but they tried.
Allowances were thus made on both sides and a certain
amount of goodwill invariably carried the day.

It was one of the little touches of luxury Dorrie always
appreciated about the Bonnard's queue. She lathered her
hands now with the richly scented cream soap and inhaled
blissfully. Civilization—this part of the city made you
realize what it was all about.

And such *hot* water. She rinsed her hands and then
rinsed out her Thermos flask. It was too early for an
attendant to be on duty, that was lucky. Dorrie took an
envelope from her handbag and shook the prepared mix-
ture of coffee granules and powdered milk into the Ther-

mos, then refilled it with the almost-boiling water.

There, that would do for an early breakfast. That and the cheese roll she had saved from her midnight snack. It would hold her comfortably until the shops opened and she could get a proper cooked breakfast. It didn't do to stint oneself when the weather was so cold. The little touches of luxury made all the difference.

Like being able to use the St Edmund's. She refilled her hot-water bottle as well and squirreled it away at the bottom of her holdall along with the Thermos. What the St Edmund's didn't know wouldn't hurt it. Not that they could possibly begrudge a bit of hot water, but it was better to be on the safe side.

She ran a comb through her hair and put on fresh lipstick. Usually, she liked to adjourn to the other room for that — the proper Powder Room, as it said on the outside door — and sit at one of the mirrored dressing-tables, but not so early. Not when the queue was still in the process of forming. That nice young couple had promised to keep her place, but she didn't trust the man immediately in front of her one iota. He'd probably think it a great joke to let someone else take her place. No, she wanted to get back quickly this morning.

And she was right. Two new people in the queue already. That was what happened with some of them. They elected to spend one last night in the comfort of their own beds and join the queue early in the morning, thus still beating the late-birds who thought it was time enough to get in the queue after the morning rush hour was over.

Were they together? It was hard to tell. For a moment, crossing the street, she had had that impression. Then, as she drew closer, she saw that they were occupying two places. So they were not together — or, not irrevocably.

The girl was English, blonde and fragile; the boy had the swarthiness of the Near or Middle East. Not that that meant anything these days. He could perfectly well have been born in this country. Especially as he was smart enough to join in the queue for the January Sale and not throw his money around paying the original asking price. Was that true British thriftiness, or just the Bazaar mentality adapting itself to a nation of shopkeepers who didn't believe in haggling but nevertheless had their own methods of doing these things?

But they had kept her place. Dorrie relaxed, realizing that she would feel much more comfortable from now on whenever she had to move from her place. The girl—and she was a *nice* girl, you could see that, even if the word as much as the concept was out of date and hopelessly old-fashioned these days—could be trusted. You could see that just by looking at her.

Smiling, Dorrie reclaimed her place in the queue, nodding ostentatious thanks to the young couple at the head of the queue to prove her right to take the place. She would even have nodded thanks to the man immediately in front of her, but he looked past her with a faint sneer, refusing to acknowledge her existence.

All right. Dorrie sniffed and turned away, busying herself with the process of wriggling back into the residual warmth of her sleeping-bag, pulling it up around her hips, propping the cushions against the wall so that she could sit up comfortably, and retrieving the hot-water bottle from her holdall and snuggling it into the small of her back.

Ah, that was better. With a faint sigh of satisfaction, she turned and smiled at the new arrivals. They regarded her solemnly, but did not seem unfriendly. Shy, poor things. Young people often were, however much they tried to pretend differently. Especially in front of their peers. But they needn't worry about *her*. Dorrie tried to project this information into the warmth of her smile.

It was up to her to take the initiative, though. She was

their elder in years, as well as in the pecking order of the queue.

'Hello,' she said. 'Just arrived, have you?'

'Yes.' The girl bit the word off impatiently.

Well, of course, it was a silly question, but one had to start a conversation some way. She ought to be more tolerant. She ought also to toss the conversational ball back.

'We've got a long wait ahead of us.' Dorrie tried again. 'We might as well get acquainted. I'm Dorothy Witson—but everybody calls me Dorrie.'

The girl looked as though she would like to call her something else. What had she said to offend her? The girl wasn't the stand-offish sort, was she? How could she be and join a queue like this? Perhaps she had private problems—but that needn't keep her from being friendly.

The silence stretched on for another awkward moment, then the girl spoke slowly, almost reluctantly.

'My name is Lucy . . .' she said. 'Lucy Bone.' It was close enough.

The old trout was still staring at her. Was she supposed to volunteer anything more? Or had she given herself away in some way?

It couldn't all come to nothing so soon!

Lucy felt a wave of despair. The idea had seemed so good, so foolproof. Too late, she realized what was wrong with it.

Other people. She hadn't thought about them, hadn't taken them into consideration at all. They had been nothing more than a painted backdrop in her imagination. But they were alive, surrounding her—and curious.

Who was it who had said *Hell is other people*?

She was trapped among them for the next five days. Along with everything else, she now had to worry about them. Their eyes watching her, their minds weighing her

up and assessing her, coming to some private opinion
which might ruin the whole plan.

She felt Sakim's hand close gently on her ankle, steady-
ing her. He was right. She mustn't go to pieces now. She
drew a deep breath, becoming aware of a new disquiet.
He had steadied her, but he had also underlined the fact
that he was one more pair of eyes studying her . . . spying
on her.

But the elderly woman ahead of her had begun speaking again. Asking another question. She frowned slightly,
trying to catch up with the bit she had missed. What was
she on about?

Oh yes. Yes, of course. The natural, the inevitable
question. But those sharp blue eyes were disconcerting.
How much did they see and register?

Uncomfortably, Lucy wriggled her foot, shaking off
Sakim's hand. Had the woman noticed?

'The coat—' she blurted quickly, trying to distract.
'The floor-length mink. It's such a bargain, isn't it?
I—I've never done anything like this before. I—I'm sorry,
I don't know the ropes at all. But it's such a bargain. So
tempting. I simply couldn't resist it. So I came along and
got into the queue really early.'

*Oh no! Oh dear! Oh, how awful. How sad. The poor,
poor child.*

How could she break it to her? And had Mr Nasty
heard?

A swift sideways glance convinced Dorrie that he had.
His sneer was more pronounced than ever. And there was
an extra degree of smugness in the self-satisfied air about
him. It was just the sort of situation he thrived on—you
could tell. It was going to be an extra delight to him to
deprive a pretty young girl of her heart's desire, snatching
it out from under her nose himself. He'd probably laugh
as he did so.

This time, the silence on *her* part had stretched on for too long. She knew, too, that her face might have betrayed her—she never had been good at keeping a neutral expression. *'Dorrie, you've got a speaking face,'* her dear old Mum had always said and it was the unfortunate truth. Already, the young girl—Lucy—was looking at her with apprehension, as though she sensed the blow that was to come.

'Oh my dear,' she said. 'I'm so sorry, so very sorry—'

'*I*—' He had heard, all right. He leaned forward now, crowding Dorrie back against the building to speak past her. '*I* am here for the floor-length mink! And I am ahead of you! I will get it! It is mine!'

'Oh!' Lucy Bone shrank back. Well, naturally, she wasn't accustomed to manners like that. Who was? It was all very well to say that he was a foreigner, but that didn't excuse him. There was no need to behave like that.

'Excuse me—' As though to prove her point, the young man behind Lucy Bone leaned forward. 'I introduce myself, yes? I am Sakim—'

'Saki—?' Dorrie asked hesitantly. The rest of the name was unintelligible.

'Sakim is enough,' he said firmly, as though he had had long experience of the trouble English tongues had with his name. 'I am here to buy the much-reduced Persian carpet.' He smiled winningly. 'For my mother. It is a surprise for her.'

'How nice!' Dorrie beamed approvingly at him. Wasn't that just what she had been thinking? *Some* foreigners were really quite nice. And planning a surprise for his mother, too. How pleased she would be. It was a lovely carpet—if you liked them that ornate—and £75, down from £1800. Another of the real bargains that made Bonnard's Sales so much more spectacular than those of its competitors.

'She will be pleased, I believe.' Sakim smiled again and

leaned back, obviously feeling that he had established his credentials, as, indeed, he had.

Lucy Bone was still looking stricken. Dorrie glanced at the man behind. Still sneering, he had dropped out of the conversation as abruptly as he had joined it. But he was still listening, she could tell that by the set of his head.

'Look, dear—' Dorrie lowered her voice and edged closer to Lucy. 'You mustn't give up. It's early days yet. He may not have any staying power. I've seen people in these queues and they come early and brag about what they're after, but a few cold nights or a bit of rain or snow and they give up and go off. You can't tell. It wouldn't surprise me to find he was one of that sort. You just sit tight and keep hoping.'

'Thank you.' Lucy smiled wanly. 'I—I suppose it *was* silly of me to imagine I'd be the only one after a bargain like that. As I told you, I—I'm not used to this sort of thing. I've never done it before.'

She had not lowered her voice and there was a muffled snort from the man on the other side of Dorrie.

'Never you mind, dear.' Dorrie rummaged in her hold-all and pulled out the Thermos flask. 'Have a nice cup of coffee with me and you'll feel better. You mustn't let it get you down. Just remember . . . *"There's many a slip"* . . .'

'I suppose so.' Lucy Bone seemed faintly cheered, perhaps at the immediate prospect of a cup of hot coffee. Dorrie wondered if she'd eaten a proper breakfast before leaving home that morning. These first-time queuers didn't realize the importance of food. Like an army marching on its stomach, a queue's stamina was derived as much from good solid food as from the anticipation of the bargains that awaited them at the end of their vigil.

The morning was growing brighter; that helped, too. Especially if there was going to be a bit of sun. Everything looked better in the sunlight. And soon the Bonnard's sales force would start clocking in and, not long after that, the customers. It was always cheerier with more people around. Even in a queue, you got bored with the limited company available, it was nice to sit back and watch the passing parade.

There was movement at the end of the street. A chauffeur-driven Rolls-Royce turned into it smoothly and glided along towards Bonnard's.

'Here comes one of the big bods now,' Dorrie announced to the others. It was not her first time in a Bonnard's queue and she knew some of the executives by sight.

She turned back to Lucy, holding out the cup of coffee, but the girl had gone.

'Thank you —' A wisp of blonde hair and the tip of a pert nose just showing at the opening of the girl's sleeping-bag. 'I — I don't think I want any coffee, after all. I'd rather try to get a bit of sleep. I — I had to get up so early this morning.'

'Best thing for you, I'm sure.' Dorrie began to drink the coffee herself. The girl would feel stronger and more hopeful after a little nap. They could put their heads together then and perhaps plot out a course of action. There were short cuts from one department to another inside Bonnard's that Mr Nasty probably didn't know anything about. There was plenty of time and the race wasn't always to the swift.

Lucy Bone ducked her head deep into the sleeping-bag, like a turtle disappearing into its shell, just as the Rolls-Royce slid past the main entrance to Bonnard's and turned the corner to pull to a halt at the Staff Entrance at the side.

CHAPTER 3

'I could always go back to New York,' Maggie Saunders said. 'That would solve all your problems.'

'It would solve nothing and you know it.' Lucien Bonnard sat down, putting the width of his desk between them. 'We've had a very pleasant holiday together, haven't we? Why do you want to spoil it now?'

'Very pleasant,' she mocked. 'With you jumping every time a telephone rang, even though no one knew where we were staying. And every time you thought I wasn't looking at you, you kept watching the door or staring out of the window. You make me feel like a jailer!'

'Maggie, I've said I'm sorry.'

'Oh God! No, Lucien, *I'm* sorry.' She perched on the end of his desk. He wished she wouldn't do that. 'It was all my fault. I shouldn't have dragged you away at a time like this.'

'No, no, Maggie, you were quite right.' He sighed heavily. 'I was sentimentalizing to think that she might want to get in touch with me at Christmas. As you pointed out, if she hadn't bothered to lift the telephone to speak to me over the past ten months—including my birthday and her birthday—it was unrealistic to expect her to do so just because it was Christmas.' His mouth twisted wryly. 'There wasn't even a card.'

'That's what I mean,' Maggie said. 'If I go, she'll come back.'

'Back to square one?' Lucien shook his head. 'As I said, that won't solve anything. She's nineteen. Another year, or two, or three—and she'll want to get married herself. She'll run off and leave me without a backward glance. Just as she has this time. Only, if you've already left me because of her, I'll be alone. And so will you. Is that your idea of a satisfactory solution?'

'No.' She slid off the desk and turned to face him squarely. 'Oh, Lucien! It's all such a mess when it ought to be so simple. You wife's been dead for six years. Who are˜ we hurting? Why shouldn't we have some happiness together?'

'Why, indeed?' He gave the Gallic shrug he had cultivated, although he had been born and bred in England and the French ancestor who had founded Bonnard's had been his great-great-grandfather. 'Perhaps, since we are back at work after our little holiday, it would be best to concentrate on work.'

'All right.' She straightened her shoulders and Lucien recognized his mistake. Such a suggestion had been the red rag to the bull. (No, no, that was incorrect — anatomically as well as literally. But to say 'red rag to the cow' did not convey the right idea, apart from being most ungallant.) He had started another hare. Rabbit? Doe? He abandoned metaphors abruptly.

What he had started was another fight — and he was in the middle of it. Again. As usual.

'You're right.' She had brought a file folder into the office with her and she pulled some papers out of it, all business now.

'The queue for the Sale,' she said. 'It's forming already. When do we put out the photo call to the newspapers to come and take their pictures?'

'We do what we have always done in the past.' He frowned. She should have read the files and familiarized herself with the routine. 'We put out the photo call on New Year's Eve so that they can take the pictures when we serve champagne to the queue — and to the photographers and journalists. They will be expecting it then. It is what Bonnard's has always done.'

'What Bonnard's has always done!' The challenging

note was back in her voice. 'The good old Victorian tradition. Don't you think it's time to drag Bonnard's, kicking and screaming though it may be, into the twentieth century? After all,' she pointed out, 'we're getting very close to the twenty-*first* century now.'

'There are still some years to go,' he said wearily. They had already been through this argument several times. 'And our Centenary Year is not the time to abandon tradition.'

'Bonnard's is just about the last store in London to hold their Sale in January. All the other stores start their sales the day after Boxing Day now.'

'We don't lose anything by it,' he said. 'People are willing to wait for Bonnard's Sale. The other sales are played out by the time ours starts.'

'That isn't the point,' she cut in impatiently. 'It's time Bonnard's caught up with modern merchandising methods. In New York—'

'In New York, the department stores now lock every door except their main entrance to try to cut down on the shoplifting losses. Is that the sort of lead you wish Bonnard's to follow?'

'You know it's not, although it wouldn't do any harm to—' She broke off, realizing that he was no longer listening.

He was remembering. They had flown to New York in the spring for the dual purpose of attending the wedding of Maggie's younger brother, which would provide an excellent opportunity of introducing him to the family and intimating their own eventual intentions, and business. The secondary purpose, of course, was to study the current methods of American merchandising and acquire any suitable luxury merchandise for Bonnard's to introduce to the Great British Public.

Lucien Bonnard had still not quite recovered from that trip. Maggie's family had been so unexpectedly daunting.

The younger ones so tall and so alarmingly self-possessed. Was it really just the American way or had he gone terribly wrong in the way he had tried to bring up his daughter? The elder members of the family had been kind, polite and self-satisfied. None of them had more than a vague idea of who he was, nor had they ever really heard of Bonnard's.

The New York department stores had been even more alarming. The plague of shoplifting in London, bad though it was, had not yet reached the pandemic proportions New York was experiencing. The horror stories were appalling, even when they were faintly funny. Despite a watchful staff, store detectives and locked doors, how *had* someone managed to strip a heavy double bedspread from the double bed in a furniture display and smuggle it out past the guards at the entrance?

Not funny at all had been the constant scenes erupting in nearly every shop. The first time it had happened, Lucien had been shocked nearly speechless.

He had been at a jewellery counter, looking for a trifle to buy for Maggie, when the screaming and shouting had started at the far end of the floor. Some of the customers wheeled about and rushed towards the scene of the excitement, others moved away from it. The girl on the counter met his questioning gaze.

'Somebody caught shoplifting,' she explained. 'They think if they yell loud enough, we'll let them go.' She gave a bored shrug. 'It doesn't work.'

He hadn't realized that New York store detectives accosted their suspects while still in the store, but it made sense. Once outside, the streets were so crowded that an agile thief might easily escape by dodging out into the traffic; the less agile could repeat the hysterical shouting they specialized in and perhaps draw some unwary Samaritans into the argument and escape while the store detective was being distracted. It was more than possible, also, that American laws operated differently and —

He had realized abruptly that his salesgirl, although still politely smiling, was watching his hands carefully. She suspected him! She actually thought that he might be in league with the person creating the disturbance, ready to snatch the jewellery that had been taken out of the case and run.

He had to fight down an impulse to bring out his credentials and explain who he was, perhaps even to offer her a job in London. Instead, he had bought more than he had intended: a peridot brooch for Maggie, an aquamarine ring for his daughter.

But Lucien Bonnard had been more shaken by the incident than he had realized. He remained shaken now. Somehow, over the past two years, all the quiet assumptions upon which his life had been based had been quietly eroded. Some latent instinct for survival deep within him had begun signalling that he must rebuild . . . or die.

'All right,' Maggie had been scribbling notations to herself on some of the papers. 'We'll get the photographers round tonight. Then what? What about the mechanics of Opening Day? Do we give them chits attesting to their place in the queue and send them home after the photographers have gone?'

'Certainly not!' Lucien was shocked. 'They enjoy the queue. Sometimes I think they enjoy the queue as much as the bargains. Go out and look at them and you'll understand. It's — it's —'

'I know,' she interrupted him. 'It's an *English thing*!'

'Precisely.' He smiled wryly.

'Which I couldn't possibly be expected to comprehend.'

'I didn't say that.'

'You were *thinking* it!'

'That's too much!' He made another of the mannered Gallic gestures that had, by now, become a part of him, an abrupt scissors motion of both hands. 'I refuse to be held accountable for what you think I'm thinking!'

'Oh, Lucien!' Abruptly she began to laugh. 'Listen to us! We sound like a couple of kids!'

'Yes.' He smiled reluctantly. 'Perhaps we are. Perhaps it's time we began acting like sensible adults, perhaps even had a child or two of our own —' Children were all hostages to fortune but, with a name and an establishment like Bonnard's, one was a perpetual hostage in oneself. More children could not put one more at risk. And, this time, things might work out more satisfactorily.

'But I thought —' She moved towards him slowly. 'You wanted to give Lucinda more time to get used to the idea.'

'She's had enough time,' Lucien Bonnard said coldly. 'She's using time against us now. She'll try to break us up by her disapproval, counting on the fact that I would value a reconciliation with her.'

It had happened before and the lady had not proved equal to Lucinda's hostility. Did Maggie know about that episode? It had happened before she appeared on the scene. All for the best, now that he had Maggie, but it had taught him something about Lucinda and about himself. He was a shopkeeper — the best shop in London, perhaps, but still a shop — and he should behave like a shopkeeper. If merchandise was faulty, one cut one's losses and replaced it. And if someone was caught deliberately damaging the merchandise — His lips tightened.

'We'll marry after the Sale,' Lucien said. Would a son be so stubborn and unyielding?

CHAPTER 4

It was a pity she had chosen to light on the floor-length mink coat but, with her accent, what else would have been believable? She could scarcely have confessed to an overwhelming passion to acquire a walk-in deep-freeze unit. And just as well she hadn't. The old hen in front had that marked out for herself—or her friends, about whom she was fiercely possessive. It amounted to the same thing.

Unfortunately, she now appeared to be numbered among those friends. From the moment Dorrie had learned that she presumably had her heart set on something she was unlikely to get, she had been firmly swept under a wing while the woman clucked at her like a mother hen with one chick.

'*Now, don't you worry and don't you give up, we'll think of something,*' had been the burden of the refrain until she'd wanted to scream. She hadn't, of course. She'd smiled with suitable gratitude and pleaded an overwhelming exhaustion so that she could slide deeper into her sleeping-bag with eyes closed when the partisan protectiveness threatened to swamp her. A person could only stand so much and this was something she had not bargained on.

Through the quilted padding of the sleeping-bag, she felt a warmth and tightness curl like a snake around one ankle. He might have meant it to be reassuring, but she wished he wouldn't do that. She twisted her ankle impatiently and felt the hand slowly withdraw. She knew that, if she were to see his face, the dark sulky look would be back on it. He didn't like being rebuffed. If there were not so many witnesses, he might have found a way to demonstrate his displeasure.

But the early-morning shoppers were beginning to arrive. Suburbanites hoping for pre-sale bargains, foreigners who had limited time and couldn't stay in London that long, people coming to try to glimpse the sale merchandise, people popping in on their way to work to pick up small items and, of course, the usual run of Bonnard's customers to whom money was no object.

Predominantly female, they clustered in the doorway waiting for the doors to open on the stroke of 9.30, twittering all the while. If only they'd be quiet! But they jabbered incessantly, talking to each other and—inevitably—to the people in the queue.

As might have been expected, Dorrie was in her glory, carrying on several conversations at once. The couple at the head of the queue also seemed to have no inhibitions about discussing their affairs with strangers. The noise level rose higher and higher, giving unwilling listeners the feeling of being trapped in the Parrot House at the Zoo.

Lucy Bone shrank still farther into her sleeping-bag, pulling the flap down over her head, trying to shut out the noise. One couldn't hear oneself think—although that was all to the good these days.

Then the noises outside her cocoon changed tempo and timbre. As sure as though she had been watching, Lucy knew what was happening.

The doorman could be seen approaching through the plate-glass entrance doors. Like an actor conscious of his big moment, Foster would move slowly and majestically, enjoying the undivided attention of those waiting in the entrance. He always slowed as he drew nearer, sometimes pausing to talk to one of the salesgirls already in position behind the cosmetic and perfumery counters flanking the main aisle.

Meanwhile, the would-be customers grew restive. It was suspected throughout Bonnard's that Foster awarded himself extra points in some private game of his own if he could reduce any of the customers to rapping sharply on the glass to try to hurry him along. He was never reprimanded, however. The others enjoyed the game, too. It was exhilarating to see how anxious the customers were to rush in and spend their money.

Evidently Foster wasn't tarrying today. The antici-patory shuffle of feet, the abrupt silence, provided a wordless commentary on his progress. He would be un-locking the doors now, slowly, giving himself an extra moment to brace himself against the rush when he flung them open. Inside the store, too, there would be the same moment of breathless hush before the rush began.

It was, as was every morning at Bonnard's, a re-creation in miniature of the Opening Day of the twice-yearly Sales. Except that you could multiply the customers by hundreds, perhaps thousands, during the days of the Sales. It would be bigger than ever for Centenary Year—even special souvenir carrier bags had been designed and would be given away free, no matter how small the purchase.

The January Sale was going to be bigger and more exciting than ever this year. Whether Bonnard's intended it, or not.

Lucy shuddered abruptly, deep in her sleeping-bag, feeling lost and cold. It was strange to be on the outside, not even looking in.

There was a final brief explosion of sound, goodbyes being called to those remaining behind in the queue, feet hurrying forward. Then silence.

'Lucy . . . Lucy . . .' The snake curled around her ankle again and tightened. 'Lucy   they are gone now . . .'

When she did not respond, the hand tightened still more and began shaking her ankle, none too gently. 'Lucy . . . come now and we will go and find something to eat. Lucy . . . do you hear me?'

Lucy remained unmoving in her sleeping-bag, feigning sleep.

There now. Dorrie nodded to herself, suspicions confirmed. She'd thought they were together the first moment she'd seen them. They hadn't paid all that much attention to each other since then, but now the boy had given it away. You don't go pawing like that at a complete stranger.

Still, no business of hers. They'd probably had a lovers' tiff. And the boy wanted to make it up now, but Lucy was still upset. You could see she was highly-strung.

Chalk and cheese, the two of them. Not that that couldn't work out quite well. She'd known some odd combinations in her time, and the funny thing was that they'd done better together than some of the couples who'd seemed to have so much in common. Maybe too much. If they'd seemed interchangeable, gender apart, to their neighbours, maybe they'd been too alike, even to themselves. A monologue with yourself could get pretty boring. You needed a bit of conflict to spice it up.

Oh dear! He had lifted his head and was looking straight at her. She hadn't been staring, had she?

'Please . . . Madam . . .' he began.

'You might as well call me Dorrie, dear,' she said. 'Start as you mean to go on. We're going to be spending a lot of days together from now on. And nights together, too.'

It was her little joke, but it left the young man looking a shade baffled and drew a contemptuous snort from the foreigner on the other side of her. Well, she'd crossed *him* off her list practically at first sight. What else could you expect from that sort?

'Yes . . . Dorrie. Thank you. I am Sakim.'

And thank heaven for that. She'd hate to try to cope with that surname he'd mumbled earlier. That was why she'd rather rushed the informality, actually. Foreigners' first names were usually more reasonable than their last and the quicker one got on first-name terms with them, the easier life was.

'Then, Dorrie . . . may I ask? You are remaining here? You are not going away?'

'Not until they open the doors for the Sale,' Dorrie declared firmly. 'I'm here on the pavement until then — and then I'm inside Bonnard's so fast all you'll see is a blur.'

'Yes. I see. I mean, right now. You are not . . .?' He gestured towards the St Edmund's. 'You are not going anywhere right now for a little while?'

'Oh!' Light dawned. 'I'm with you now.'

'With me?' He looked unnerved and faintly embarrassed.

'No, no, I'm not going with you. I mean, I understand you.' Oh dear, it was getting to be heavy weather. And Little Madam, tucked into her sleeping-bag, was quite plainly going to be of no help at all.

'You mean you'd like to go and freshen up and get a bite to eat.'

'Yes, yes,' he said with eager relief. 'That is it.'

'And you want me to keep your place in the queue for you. Of course I will. We all do that for each other,' she explained gently. As this was the first time he had ever queued for anything, he was bound to be unfamiliar with the etiquette.

'That is it,' he said again. 'Precisely. Most kind of you.' He scrambled to his feet, then hesitated, looking down at the closed sleeping-bag.

'She'll be all right,' Dorrie said. 'I wouldn't be surprised if she weren't still asleep when you get back.'

Far from reassuring him, the thought seemed to upset him. His face changed, the ingratiating smile replaced by a brief murderous glare that sent Dorrie recoiling involuntarily.

'It is nothing to me,' he denied unconvincingly. As

swiftly as it had disappeared the ingratiating smile returned and he bobbed his head in exaggerated gratitude. 'Most kind of you.'

'Not at all,' Dorrie said coldly. 'I'd do it for anyone.'

He frowned nervously, seeming to sense that he had lost ground in some indefinable way.

Dorrie became very busy hunting through her holdall for something. When she finally looked up, he was turning the corner heading towards the cheaper district where small lunch counters abounded.

Dorrie turned and looked at the sleeping-bag thoughtfully. 'You can come out now, dear,' she said. 'He's gone.'

By lunch-time, Maggie was shoulder high in the reference books spilling across her desk. There were still more that she needed, but she had the gloomy suspicion that they didn't exist. It had taken concerted raids on libraries, private collections and antiquarian booksellers to amass this many. And still the information they provided was inadequate.

She lifted an ornate pectoral cross in white enamel, studded with deep purple amethysts, outlined in green peridots and yellow citrines, surmounted by a gleaming gold crown and suspended from a long heavy chain which was 22-karats if it was one. It matched no illustration in any of the reference books. Where had he got it from? Which grateful precariously-crowned head had bestowed it in lieu of the currency which should have been paid for his purchases?

'And God bless our greedy founder,' she muttered, letting it fall back on the desk top.

'Having difficulties, my love?' Lucien smiled from the doorway.

'Not more than a few dozen.' She smiled back. 'But I'm trying to look upon it as a challenge.'

So far as she and the Publicity Department were con-

cerned, the January Sale was all over bar the shouting and
the final tallies rung up on the tills. They were deep in the
Exhibition being mounted for February—which would
provide excitement for a normally dull month and then
carry on through the Tourist Season until late autumn.
An exhibition of all the medals, awards, orders, gifts and
sundries presented by grateful customers who, just coinci-
dentally, happened to number among them most of the
tinpot monarchs of the pre-and-post-World War I
civilization.

'When we were children, we didn't believe these were
real.' Lucien leaned over her shoulder and stirred them
with a casual forefinger, turning them into a glittering
whirlpool of diamonds, rubies, sapphires, zircons, tur-
quoises, garnets, moonstones, emeralds, opals, gold,
silver, enamel—

'Lucien—stop it!' She caught his hand. 'I've just begun
to identify some of them and you're mixing them all up
again.'

'Good work! Have you discovered who these are yet?' He
picked up a gold frame encrusted with garnets and pin-
point diamonds. Inside the frame, a sad and solemn sepia
couple stared out with regal resignation as though they
had already glimpsed the fate that awaited them. Their
signatures were indecipherable. 'I've always wondered.'

'Minor royalty, I'd guess. A Grand Duke and Duchess—
perhaps even less.'

'Snob!' he laughed. 'I can see I'm bringing a worthy
successor to Great-Great-Grandfather Lucien into the
family.'

'I'm not quite that bad,' she said. She disentangled a
turquoise, garnet and seed pearl monstrosity and matched it
up with the white card on which preliminary notes were
written. 'Good old Great-Great-Grandfather Lucien.
Didn't he ever make *any* of these royal deadbeats pay cash
on the nail?'

'Good old Great-Great-Grandfather Lucien,' he echoed with the amused tolerance one can afford to cherish for a highly successful ancestor. 'He dearly loved his little baubles.'

It was a fact which had rapidly become well known throughout the Balkan and mid-European kingdoms. The bestowal of a suitably gaudy Order Third Class, or even Fourth Class, was sufficient collateral for the running up of a bill of considerable size at the most modern and exclusive London Departmental Store. For countries endowed with a gold mine or two and plentiful supplies of amber, garnet and semi-precious stones but a permanent cash crisis, the amiable and excellent Lucien Bonnard was a most understanding purveyor of modern luxuries. *Naturellement*, one wished to reward such devotion with a trifling Order in exchange for an order. Such was the good M. Bonnard's delight in these simple tokens of royal affection that he frequently tore up the bills—which he had little hope of collecting, in any case—and a warm glow of mutual admiration pervaded all.

'The funny thing is that the old boy was right,' Lucien said. 'He could afford to write off the debts and these baubles he collected have kept pace with inflation in their intrinsic value alone. Their historic value is incalculable. Most of these countries don't even exist any more.'

'I know,' Maggie said. 'I've been trying to trace them. I'm amazed to find they ever existed. I always thought all those Ruritanian names were invented by romantic novelists and bad playwrights. Bohemia, Moldavia, Croatia, Montenegro—even Transylvania—for God's sake! I'd always thought Bram Stoker made that up! At least, I did until they started running tours there. But half of these other places I've never even heard of.

'Not many people have. Most of these countries were swept away during or after the First World War and the world has kept on changing rapidly ever since. After the

Second World War, the ones that were left wound up
behind the Iron Curtain with their names changed yet
again.' He frowned down at the sparkling display. 'These
things are really museum pieces now.'

'We'll have the Art Department draw a large map of
Europe in the Victorian Era,' Maggie decided crisply.
'We can mount it over the display cases. Perhaps with
coloured ribbons running from the country on the map to
the decoration in the display case. It could be quite effec-
tive—and it would save the customers from feeling as
uneducated as I feel at not knowing my early European
geography.'

'No one could be expected to keep up with Euro-
pean—or African—geography these days. Even the map-
makers must be hard-pushed to realign boundaries and
change names fast enough.' He patted her shoulder. 'So
stop worrying about your intellectual deficiencies and
come and have lunch. The car is waiting at the side
entrance.'

'Good.' She pushed back her chair and stood up. This
brought into view the contributions from British royalty.
A line of carved and painted coats-of-arms leaning
against the wall along the baseboard, each bearing the
'By Appointment' legend. Bonnard's 'By Appointment to
HM Queen Victoria' and all down the Royal line to the
present day. Not so flashy as the bejewelled Orders from
Mittel-European monarchs, but equally valuable. Sover-
eigns who can afford to pay their bills needn't be so lavish
with their tributes to tradesmen.

Maggie turned, laughing, to remark on this to Lucien,
but found him unusually sombre, looking at the corner of
the desk where a handful of more recent medals, drab in
comparison with the splendours of a bygone age, were
clustered together. These were predominantly British and
had been earned in quite different ways by his father in
World War I and the elder brother who had not survived

World War II to inherit Bonnard's: the Distinguished Flying Cross, the Croix de Guerre, the George Medal, the Victoria Cross. The Bonnard family had served Crown and Country well in more ways than one. The proud array would wind up the Exhibition in a special display case of their own.

'Come on.' She touched his arm gently, calling him back to the present. 'Help me to get these all back in the safe before we go to lunch.'

'You're very conscientious.' His tone was complimentary. It was gratifying to know that the woman he would marry had a proper concern for the family heirlooms.

'I always was.' She began gathering up the jewelled pieces, disentangling the gold chains he had so carelessly scrambled together. 'That's why this Exhibition waits in the safe until the January Sale is over. It's too valuable and too tempting. The Security people will have enough on their hands with the Sale. I want their undivided attention when we unveil this Exhibition.'

CHAPTER 5

It was an unsettled afternoon. Not just the weather,
although that was bad enough, chill and grey with an
occasional flurry of sleet mixed with snow. The old year
was flinging itself out in a fit of petulant spite.

Things weren't any better in the queue. Lucy Bone and
Sakim had not made up their spat and the girl had spent
most of the day huddled in her sleeping-bag. That, in
itself, was unsettling as well as being bitterly disappoint-
ing. Dorrie had had such hopes of the Bonnard's queue; it
had promised to be a pleasant interlude with charming
people. And here she was, stuck between a sneering bad-
tempered foreigner, who had taken twenty-four hours to
disclose that his name was Zoltan Something-or-other,
and a sulking little madam who was not disposed to be
friendly.

Still, it was early days yet. Lucy Bone couldn't hide
away in there for ever, she'd have to come out some time,
else she'd be bored to tears long before the Sale started.
And her odd young man *did* seem willing to be
friendly—if a bit awkward about it. Trying to make up
for her bad manners, it was obvious. It was a shame
they'd had their little misunderstanding just at this time,
but no doubt they'd sort it out before too much more time
had passed.

No, the real cause for concern was just beyond Sakim.
The next place in the queue—and who was taking it?
That was what they'd all like to know.

Since mid-morning there had been a constant coming
and going at that spot. Someone had joined the queue,
that was certain. But who?

One minute there was a young man setting down a

camp stool, bed roll, package of paperbacks and all sorts of bits and pieces, for all the world as though he were about to settle in for the duration.

And then, the next minute he was gone. Two girls, looking so much alike they might have been twins, were there instead.

But before anyone could begin making overtures to them, they'd hared off and someone else had taken their place.

And that was the way it had gone all day, like some mad variation on Musical Chairs. They all had one thing in common: each of them clutched a clipboard full of papers which they were constantly riffling through and studying.

No, not just that. There was one other thing they all had in common: stand-offish, the lot of them.

Inevitably, the others began to suspect the worst. These newcomers couldn't be an entire commune thinking they could all squeeze into one place, could they? It was a question that grew more and more worrisome as the day wore on and strangers came and went.

Even Mr Nasty Zoltan was forced into declaring a reluctant partisanship with the long-standing queue members.

'These people—' he complained. 'Who are they? How many are they? What do they want?'

Questions every one of them would dearly love to be able to answer.

'They do not speak, except among themselves,' Sakim said. As the one nearest to them, he had been listening avidly, but had to admit, 'I do not understand what they are saying. It makes no sense.' He wriggled his shoulders uneasily. 'They speak of shooting all the time.'

The sleeping-bag twitched convulsively and a blonde curly head emerged, turtlelike. 'Oooh.' An arm appeared on either side of the head as she sighed and stretched, blinking although there was little light to speak of. There had been no sun all day and the street lights had come on hours ago, as had the lights in the display windows.

'Oooh,' Lucy Bone yawned again. 'I was so exhausted . . . how long have I slept? What time is it?'

'It is past six,' Sakim said. 'The store closed more than half an hour ago.'

He seemed to have told her more than he had actually said. She smiled faintly and wriggled half way out of her sleeping-bag, sitting up against the building. 'I think I'm hungry.'

Impassively he offered her a bar of chocolate.

'I'm hungrier than that!' She waved it away and looked around, eyes widening in improbable innocence. 'Are there any decent places to eat around here?' She glanced towards the St Edmund's and away again. 'Not too expensive?'

'As it happens,' Sakim said. 'I have myself found an excellent place earlier in the day. It is nearby, the food is good and the price reasonable. If you would like me to show you—?'

'Yes, please. It sounds just right.' Lucy Bone extended her hand and let Sakim pull her to her feet.

They walked off together, having fooled no one but themselves if they thought anyone had been taken in by that stilted little performance. The rest of the queue watched them depart, then turned to each other with raised eyebrows.

'Now what do you suppose all that was in aid of?' Dorrie voiced the thought in all their minds.

'It was certainly rather odd,' Faye Moore said and her husband nodded agreement.

'Perhaps they wish it established that this is the first time they have met. Here in Bonnard's queue.' Zoltan gave a peculiarly Mittel-European shrug. 'It is practically a guarantee of respectability in this country, no?'

'Bonnard's *does* have one of the nicest queues in town.' Dorrie carefully refrained from looking at him. 'Usually.'

'You see—' He spread his hands. 'They obviously feel that they can disarm parents who might not approve by telling them that they have become acquainted here. It is as good as a proper introduction.'

'Well, not quite,' Dorrie said. 'But it would be better than admitting that they'd first met in a disco—which is probably what happened.'

'And the young man is buying the Persian rug to propitiate his mother, who is undoubtedly extremely old-fashioned and has, perhaps, even begun the bargaining for an aranged marriage.' Zoltan had obviously decided their story to his own satisfaction.

'And you think Lucy is getting—' Dorrie broke off at his frown and amended hastily— '*Wanted* to get the mink coat for *her* mother?'

'No . . .' His frown deepened. 'With a daughter, it is usually the father who is the more difficult parent.' His face cleared.

'She wants it for herself,' he decided. He nodded in satisfaction. 'One can see that she is selfish and accustomed to getting her own way.'

He had jumped on that idea because it excused his own selfishness—that was as plain as the nose on your face. Dorrie shivered with distaste. It was unfair that he had beaten poor Lucy to his place in the queue by just a few hours. *He* was the selfish one, if ever anybody was. It was nicer and fairer to queue for something you wanted personally and were going to use yourself than to queue up for an item you only intended to resell at a profit. There was no law against it—more's the pity—but it wasn't really *right.*'

Well, no point in arguing with that sort of person. But it was one more black mark against him. Dorrie turned away slightly and became aware that there was now a single figure occupying the place in the queue directly behind the two empty places she had promised to hold.

He looked vaguely familiar and she thought he was probably the boy who had taken the place in the first instance, but there had been so many comings and goings that it was hard to be certain.

He was alone, however, and regarding the others in the queue with a lively and friendly curiosity. He seemed to sense that she was looking at him and, moving his head abruptly, met her gaze.

'Hello there,' he said. 'It looks as though we're going to be neighbours for the next few days.'

'So it does,' she agreed cautiously. 'Twice removed, that's to say.'

'I'm Tony—' He stretched a hand across the unoccupied places. 'Tony Adair.'

'Dorrie,' she admitted. He *did* seem an improvement on the one on the other side of her, and he *was* English. 'Dorrie Witson.' He had a good firm handshake and a nice smile. She began to approve of him. Of course, the vital question was yet to be answered.

'Er . . .' He felt it, too. His gaze moved past her, resting speculatively on Zoltan, then on Faye and Tim. 'Have you been here long?'

'Since ten o'clock last night,' Dorrie said proudly.

'And there were already people ahead of you. That makes me a real late-comer. I thought I'd be in plenty of time if I started queueing today but . . .' He looked at the vacant places between them. 'I'm afraid I miscalculated. I hope I'm not too late.'

'You might not be,' Dorrie did not pretend to misunderstand, she was as anxious to know the answers as he was. 'We're not all here after the same thing, you know.'

'There *is* that.' He brightened, but glanced around half suspiciously. There were a lot of them like that. They thought whatever they were after was so irresistible that they hated to admit what it was, in case the others hadn't noticed it before but would immediately add it to the shopping list once their attention had been drawn to it. They couldn't believe that their coveted item might be of no interest at all to other people.

'I'm here for the walk-in fridge-freezer,' she confided, hoping to prod him into a similar confidence. 'Not for myself, of course, it's much too big for me, but my friends are going to be partners in a pub and it will be no end of use to them. They can't spare the time to queue themselves, what with Sandra having to look after the children and George having to work, and I've got nothing but time, so here I am.'

'Division of labour,' he nodded. 'We've been doing that ourselves today. You've probably noticed.'

'There did seem to be a lot of coming and going,' she admitted, careful not to sound censorious.

'Yes, well, there shouldn't be so much of that from now on,' he said. 'It was just getting all the details finalized so that I could join the queue and the others could go ahead and keep to schedule without me. I may have rather a lot of visitors, though.'

'Oh, no one will mind that.' It was not the confidence she had hoped to elicit, but it would do for a start. 'It makes it rather nice to see new faces once in a while. Smiling faces,' she added, not caring if the sour-faced foreigner behind heard. It might do him good, in fact, to realize that people expected a bit of pleasantness when they were thrown together for a long period of time. 'Your friends seemed quite nice. Although they didn't mix much.'

'They have a lot on their minds,' he said.

'They *did* seem busy.' She waited expectantly.

'Yes, we—' He hesitated a moment, then plunged ahead. 'We're shooting a film. There's a lot to do.'

'Aaah!' That explained a lot of things. Dorrie rapidly

reviewed the prize bargains. 'Then you must be queuing for the cine-camera!'

'Er, yes.' He seemed unsettled by her swift deduction. 'That's right. *And* all the associated equipment. It will go a long way towards setting us up as a professional operating unit. Not that we're not professional,' he explained quickly. 'We are, but we haven't studio backing. We're shooting this off our own hook and a lot depends on it. Like our future careers.'

'Isn't that wonderful!' Behind her, Dorrie was aware of a rustle of relief from the others. The pleasant newcomer was no competition for any of their goals. There was not going to be a duplication of the awkward situation that had already developed.

'You see—' The bars were down now and he was growing enthusiastic. 'We're well along with this film—it's a Documentary. Everyone starts out that way. Practically everyone. It's the easiest to get backing for. But with better equipment—' He turned and looked longingly into the display window.

It just went to show. She'd hardly noticed the stuff herself. But, sure enough, there in the far corner of the window, was set up an expensive-looking camera on a tripod, with all sorts of bits and pieces hanging around it. She'd thought it was as much a way of showing off the main items as anything else. The camera was aimed at the exquisitely-gowned dummies reclining on the living-room suite, thus calling attention to them, in case anyone had overlooked them. It had never particularly occurred to her that the camera equipment was for sale, but now that the young man had pointed it out, she noticed the discreet sale tags inconspicuously distributed around the display.

'Not just the best camera available,' Tony Adair said reverentially, 'but a zoom lens, a pick-up boom and mike . . . do you realize there's a whole studio in miniature there? And it's up for grabs!'

'I suppose it wasn't a very popular item,' Dorrie said. You could see that it would only appeal to the most specialized tastes.

'What?' He looked at her as though she had just lapsed into raving blasphemy.

'Else it wouldn't be on sale,' she pointed out.

'Oh, I suppose not.' It was a new idea and he examined it suspiciously, obviously still not sure that he wasn't being lulled into a false sense of security.

'I mean—' She realized that she had been remiss in her self-appointed duty; he still didn't know that his ambition was safe. 'I mean, you're the only one in the queue for it. So far. But you're the first, so it's safely yours.'

'Is it?' His face lit up. 'You're sure?' He couldn't believe his good luck. 'When I saw so many others ahead of me, I was afraid—'

'Faye and Tim—' She nodded towards them and they nodded back, beaming at the newcomer. 'They're after the living-room suite. Mr Zoltan—' The nods were cooler, but still cordial. 'He wants the floor-length mink coat.'

'And the silver fox jacket,' Zoltan said quickly, glaring as though he suspected this might be snapped up by anyone in films.

'Yes, that, too,' Dorrie amended coldly. He was shameless about parading his greed. She waited, but he did not go on to explain the full extent of his cleverness; he usually went on to tell everyone just how much of a profit he hoped to make from reselling his bargains.

'And the others?' Tony Adair prompted her. 'These two immediately in front of me?'

'Oh, well.' Dorrie was curiously reluctant to put it into words. 'Sakim is after the Persian carpet. He wants it for a present for his mother.' She halted, unhappy about going on.

'What about the girl?' He was not letting her off. 'What does she want?'

'Oh, dear! Well . . . I'm afraid . . . she came to queue for the floor-length mink coat.'

'Oh, I say!' He whistled softly. 'That *is* awkward, isn't it?' His eyes met hers with sympathetic comprehension. 'And you're right in the middle, aren't you?'

CHAPTER 6

The St Edmund's Hotel had its instructions. They were the same at the end of every December and came through direct from the Chairman's Office at Bonnard's. They were always a pleasure to carry out.

The champagne had been chilled and at quarter to midnight was transferred to ice-buckets. Glasses were waiting on trays and a running check was instituted on the state of the queue across the street.

Inevitably, some New Year revellers gate-crashed the queue each year, but the orders from Bonnard's encompassed them. They were to be treated as *bona fide* members of the queue. The glasses of champagne would be offset against the goodwill gained and considered cheap at the price. There were never too many of them and they were often the offspring of valued customers, who would grow into good solid customers in their turn, with fond recollections of the New Year's Eve they had 'put one over' on dear old Bonnard's.

Bonnard's and, indeed, the St Edmund's, felt that anyone who joined the queue, however briefly, in the sort of weather usual at the midnight between December and January had earned their champagne.

Tonight was worse than ever. A bone-chilling wind blew a fine spray of icy sleet down the street. The forecast was for more of the same, with the temperature dropping another three degrees before dawn. It would seem more appropriate to serve hot cholcolate laced with rum, or coffee with brandy, rather than iced champagne. However, the traditions must be observed.

Considering the state of the weather and the undesirability of watered champagne, the glasses were

placed upside down on the tray for the first lap of their
journey and not one bottle was opened beforehand.

At five minutes to midnight, the front door of the St
Edmund's swung ceremonially open and the small procession crossed the street to Bonnard's with somewhat more
haste than was strictly seemly.

'Here they come!' Dorrie announced triumphantly to
the semi-somnambulant members of the queue. 'I told
you they always did!'

'And you were right!' Tony Adair wriggled free of his
sleeping-bag, beaming. 'Let's hear it for them! Hip-hip—'

'HOORAY!' The queue, which had been genteelly
roistering for the past couple of hours, responded wholeheartedly.

'Hip-hip—'

'HOORAY!' They were struggling to their feet now,
trying to free themselves from blankets and scarves.

'Hip-hip—'

A sudden increase in the density of the downpour broke
the stately lines of the procession and sent the waiters
scurrying for the shelter of the overhang protecting Bonnard's pavement.

'HOORAY!' With gusts of laughter, the queue greeted
the St Edmund's Samaritans.

'It is the pleasure of Bonnard's, and, may I say, the St
Edmund's—' Mopping the sleet from his face with the
damp towel which had been draped over his forearm, the
major domo gave his accustomed speech. 'And so we have
the very great pleasure to wish all of you good people a
very Happy New Year.'

Deftly the waiter upended the glasses; the major domo
transferred the towel to the neck of the first champagne
bottle and began worrying the cork with his thumbs.

Dorrie found herself swaying gently. She would be glad
to sit down again, but of course you had to stand up for
the New Year's toast. And for the linking of hands and

singing of 'Auld Lang Syne' — although 'New Lang Syne' would be more like it, since they'd none of them known each other for more than a couple of days — with the possible exception of the young couple immediately behind her.

Dorrie cut short a bibulous little giggle. She *wasn't* tiddly — not really. But how much had she had to drink? Not all that much — it was the variety.

George and Sandra — they spoiled her dreadfully — had stopped by earlier in the evening with a bottle of brandy as a New Year present for her. So, naturally, she had offered it around. Well, it was a freezing night, wasn't it?

Of course that had started off the others. Everyone had taken it in turn to stand a round. Which was fine, except that Faye and Tim had passed round gin, Zoltan had brought along slivovitz, Lucy Bone's partiality was scotch, Sakim had produced something called arak, and Tony Adair had admitted — and proved — that the currently fashionable tipple in his group was Canadian rye.

Never mind, it was New Year's Eve. It was practically a civic duty to be a little bit sloshed on New Year's Eve.

There were, of course, two or three couples in evening dress who had recently attached themselves to the end of the queue, clustering together, accepting and offering nothing. It always happened. Freeloaders who knew, or suspected, that free champagne would be on tap at midnight. It was too bad that people always abused privileges like that. Not that they didn't pay for it in the end. Judging from the expressions on the girls' faces, as they shivered in their inadequate wraps, those young men who thought they were so smart were going to be looking for new girl-friends in the New Year. It was to be hoped that a couple of glasses of free champagne were worth it to them.

'Oooh!' Dorrie giggled as the tray of champagne glasses was held before her. 'I'm not really sure that I ought to. I mean, how does champagne mix with everything else we've been drinking tonight?'

'Magnificently, dear lady!' Zoltan's glass swooped aloft, amazingly not spilling a drop. 'It is legend that champagne mixes with everything.'

'Well, then.' She allowed herself to be persuaded and took a glass from the tray.

'In any case, it does not matter,' Zoltan added. 'Bonnard's does not open on New Year's Day. We shall be able to rest undisturbed in the morning.'

'The staff work,' Lucy Bone said unexpectedly. 'It's one of their busiest days. They get most of the ticketing done for the Sale.' She sipped at her champagne, swamped by a wave of nostalgia. It was one of the busiest days, but also one of the happiest. Without any customers underfoot, the Bonnard's staff worked as a joyous laughing team. They were paid overtime for working on that day and the canteen did an extra special meal; wine was served with the compliments of the Bonnard family and the aisles rang with jokes and laughter while everyone worked at top speed to prepare for the Sale.

'As I said—' Zoltan gave a shrug, dismissing the staff as negligible. 'They will use the service entrance. We shall not be disturbed.'

'Of course, the service entrance.' Instinctively, Lucy Bone's hand crept to the chain around her neck and the key suspended from it—the most exclusive latch key in town. She was abruptly aware of Sakim's warning growl and dropped her hand quickly.

'This way, people!' A blast of light exploded in their faces.

'That's fine. Let's have another one, please. Raise your glasses—' Another flashbulb set them blinking, yellow and blue lights dotting their vision even when they closed their eyes.

Lucy Bone flinched and turned away. There had been

other photographers earlier, but she and Sakim had seen them coming and managed to escape. They had been from the newspapers obviously bent on faking the New Year's Toast pictures so that they wouldn't have to interrupt their own festivities by coming out in the cold at the proper time. It had been easy to evade them and then to outwait them. They had delayed for a short time, hoping the missing queue members would return, but eventually had given up and had the others close up so that it could not be noticed that not everyone was there.

Dorrie had been sympathetic when they had returned. 'You missed having your picture taken,' she told Lucy. 'A shame. Your mother would have enjoyed seeing you in the paper.'

'My mother's dead,' Lucy had said shortly.

'Oh, I'm sorry—'

'It's all right. It was years ago.' But Lucy felt the tears rising behind her eyes. It was not all right. It never had been. It never would be.'

'I didn't let anyone mention anything about you.' Curiously, Dorrie seemed to understand. She wasn't a bad old duck.

'I thought it would be better not. If the newspapers heard that you were after the same thing as him—' She had jerked her head towards Zoltan. Well, they'd have played it up, wouldn't they? They always do. And we don't want that. Least said, soonest mended—' She gave an oddly rakish wink. 'You can't tell what will happen until it's all over. He might give up and go home. If we get a cold snap. Or something—'

Instead of being irritated, as she might have expected, Lucy found herself curiously comforted. The old duck didn't understand a thing—how could she?—but there was so much sheer good will emanating from her that it was impossible not to feel it and, however unwilling, respond.

'Thank you.' She had returned the smile. 'I—I'd have hated to have the newspapers make a thing of this.'

'No, no! This way! Look this way!' The 'Please' was added as an afterthought. 'You don't want to ruin the picture, do you?'

That was precisely what she did want. Under cover of being obliging, Lucy swivelled rapidly just as the flashbulb exploded. That ought to produce a nice unidentifiable blur.

'Let's try again, shall we?' The photographer pleaded, with nerve-grinding patience. 'That was probably okay, but let's try it one more time. For good luck.'

'You got that, did you?' Tony Adair moved forward with professional interest. 'What are you using?'

'Ah—' The photographer expanded, recognizing a fellow enthusiast. 'I'm using a setting of—' His voice dropped, he held out his camera for inspection, the two men lapsed into incomprehensible jargon as the camera was passed back and forth between them.

Wisely, the St Edmund's people recharged the champagne glasses.

'There go the bells!' Dorrie remained alert. 'It's midnight! Happy New Year!'

'Happy New Year!' Automatically they raised glasses to each other as the bells chimed out the hour.

The lightning flash caught them by surprise. They had almost forgotten the photographer, assuming him to be too preoccupied to take a picture at that moment.

'That's great,' he encouraged them. 'Let's have one last one now—just to make sure.'

'Excuse me.' Zoltan frowned at him. 'But I did not catch the name of your newspaper. It is a national one? These pictures will appear—where?'

'Oh, er . . .' For the first time, the photographer appeared embarrassed, diminished somehow. 'I'm not with a paper. Not just now. I'm with Bonnard's. The

Publicity Department. These pictures are mainly for our records. Although, of course, we'll send them out with captions for our next Press Release on the Sale. But I couldn't tell you which papers might pick them up and use them. Perhaps all of them,' he added unconvincingly.

'And perhaps not!' Zoltan drained his glass, replaced it on the waiting tray, and sat down with an air of finality.

'Oh now, don't be like that,' Dorrie said, annoyed. You might just know he'd turn sulky if he thought he wasn't getting the right sort of attention.

'Come on, now — *Should auld acquaintance be forgot . . .*' With horror, she heard her unsteady treble rise into the night. Oh dear, she *had* had too much. No two ways about it —

'*And never brought to mind . . .*' But the others didn't seem to mind. In fact, they seemed quite glad someone had started the singing. They linked hands and, between them, Dorrie and Tim jerked Zoltan to his feet to join in the chain.

'*Should auld acquaintance be forgot . . .*' Lucy was abruptly aware that Tony Adair had pushed in between her and Sakim and was holding her hand. Sakim would be infuriated. She'd have to pay for that later — even though it wasn't her fault. She tried to disengage her hand, but he held fast. The photographer was going to take another picture, too.

'*And days of auld lang syne . . .*' Stupid sentimental tears were suddenly too close. Lucy Bone raised her chin defiantly and stared directly into the lens. Well, why not? They'd have to know some time. That was the point of the whole thing. Or, rather, one of the points.

'*For auld lang syne, my dear . . .*' The melody filled the night, the flashbulbs sent out waves of sheet lightning, the queue were caught up in the moment.

'*For auld lang syne . . .*' The St Edmund's waiters began a strategic withdrawal while the others were unnoticing. The champagne bottles were empty and it was obvious that the people in the queue had enough supplies of their own to keep them happy for quite some time yet. Bonnard's and the St Edmund's had done their duty for another year.

'*We'll tak a cup o' kindness yet* . . .' Lucy Bone choked and stopped singing. But no one noticed.

CHAPTER 7

'Are you sure?' Maggie scrabbled in her top drawer for the magnifying glass, usually only brought into play to check the detail of a reduced line drawing in one of the ads. It wasn't really needed, but the search gave her a moment's respite while she tried to decide what to do.

'Certain as I can be, Miss Saunders.' The man on the other side of her desk, staring down at the glossy prints, was sympathetic. It was not a decision he would like to make himself — which was why he had dumped the problem in her lap.

'I thought she looked familiar, just from the glimpses I got of her in the queue the other day. Of course she's changed some over the past year or so, but girls do at that age, don't they?' Foster, with no doors to guard today, had come in to help out with the pre-Sale activity. For that matter, they all had. Today was like a big family party, all Bonnard's people, undisturbed by customers, working busily and looking forward to the splendid late afternoon luncheon which turned the whole day into more a New Year's Party than a strictly workday.

Force of habit had driven Foster automatically to check the front doors and the state of the queue. He liked to see it grow as more and more people joined it the closer the day of the Sale came. The face he had seen — or thought he had seen — among the semi-comatose forms had sent him rushing to the Publicity Office to verify his suspicions against the photographs always taken of the queue enjoying their traditional midnight champagne.

'You could call Mrs Kane down,' he offered. 'Just to make sure.' Angela Kane, Lucien Bonnard's private secretary, was the last Court of Appeal before the matter had to go to Lucien himself.

She would know, if anyone would. Maggie picked up the internal phone and dialled the extension.

'Angie, could you come down here a moment?' She listened in silence to the surprised protests at the other end. It seemed that Lucien was about to start dictating almost immediately.

'It will only take a minute.' Maggie hesitated. 'It *is* urgent.'

Foster shook his head as Maggie indicated a chair and continued standing before her desk. They waited in silence, not needing to share their thoughts.

They watched in silence as Angela Kane crossed the room to stare down at the pictures on the desk. She was the one to break the silence.

'Oh God!' She shook her head despairingly. 'Lucien will have to know!'

They both looked at Maggie. She realized wryly that it was a tacit admission of her as yet unannounced new position: she was—or was about to be—one of the family. One of the Bonnards. It was, therefore, her duty to break the news to Lucien.

It was an acknowledgement she could have done without.

'All right.' Maggie pushed back her chair and gathered up the blurred photograph and the other one. The beautifully clear one with the girl staring straight in to the camera lens and holding her glass aloft in a mocking toast.

'All right,' she said again, as though they had been arguing with her. 'All right, I'll tell him.'

'I don't understand.' Lucien Bonnard dropped the photographs on to his desk, bowed his head and shielded his eyes briefly with one hand.

'We thought you ought to know,' Maggie said inadequately.

'Quite right.' He dropped his hand and gave her a glacial unnerving smile, not really seeing her at all, not seeing anything except the bright mocking face looking up from the photograph.

'I don't understand,' he repeated. 'What can she hope to gain by this? What does she want?'

Before Maggie could speak, he answered his own question.

'She wants to humiliate me.'

He understood all too well. He had just proved it.

'She wants to cause a scandal.'

'Well,' Maggie said judiciously, 'it isn't done — not even in the States. It's sort of like those contests where the rules always state that the contest isn't open to employees of the firm or their families, or employees of the advertising agency and their families. It isn't strictly illegal, but it —'

'It leaves a nasty taste in the mouth.' Lucien looked as though his taste buds were shrivelling and protesting under the impact of a strange and sinister new flavour. One which was unlikely to find favour in the market-place.

Maggie nodded, avoiding his eyes. It was ridiculous that she should feel so guilty. It was *his* store, *his* daughter — none of this was her fault, but still she felt guilty. It was unfair, it was wrong that she should be made to feel this way.

Worse, it meant that Lucinda Bonnard was winning. In this strange unequal war the girl had declared, where she set the rules, chose the battlefield, decided the weapons, she was almost inevitably bound to win. And yet, she could not be allowed to win.

If she won, Lucien perished. The final outcome was as simple and as inexorable as that.

'She could have anything in the store she wanted.' Lucien seemed to be pleading. 'She knows that. All she had to do is ask. She needn't even ask me, if she doesn't

want to speak to me. All she'd have to do is to walk in and
take what she wants. The staff know her, they'd let her
walk away with anything she wanted and simply send me
an indent for it. They'd know I'd pass it. Why should she
go out to spend days in the queue?'

He had already answered that question, but Maggie
did not remind him of it.

'We could disperse the queue,' Maggie suggested.
'Other stores are doing it these days. We could give them
chits according to their place in the queue and reserve the
items they've queued for until they come in to pick them
up when the Sale opens.'

'That would only make the situation worse.' Lucien put
his finger on the weakness in the plan even as it belatedly
occurred to her. 'She'd have the chit then, and we'd have
no way of proving that she had ever been in the queue at
all. This way, at least people can see that she's been queuing the full length of time. So there's a limit —' his mouth
twisted wryly— 'to the amount of favouritism we can be
accused of showing.'

'Oh, Lucien—' Maggie stopped herself just in time.
Too much criticism of his daughter was not the way to his
heart. In this situation, she was the outsider, the intruder,
the one who must always tread warily.

'Lucien . . .' She crossed to stand behind his chair, letting her arms encircle him, her cheek rest against the top
of his head. It was safer to put nothing into words.

He allowed it briefly, then wriggled his shoulders impatiently, freeing himself from her embrace.

She moved away quickly, putting the desk between
them again. He did not appear to notice. His face ex-
pressionless, he sat looking down at the photographs, lost
in some distant memories, disappeared into a world in
which she could not reach him.

'I'll start some enquiries,' Maggie said briskly, heading
for the door. 'If we can find out what she's queuing for,

that might give us some clue as to how to deal with the situation.'

'That's fine.' It was an acknowledgement of her desire to be helpful, not carrying any hope that she could possibly be successful. 'You do that.'

Fury rose in her; he was halfway defeated already. And all because he was allowing himself to be. Why didn't he fight back? If only he'd lose his temper, it would be a start.

'Well, anyway—' She paused in the doorway and flung it at him recklessly.

'At least you'll know where she is tonight!'

CHAPTER 8

It might not be fair of her, but personally she blamed the slivovitz.

Dorrie managed to twitch one eye open and instantly regretted it deeply.

Scotch and brandy were well known to be medicinal. A drop of gin never hurt anybody. The arak had been so strange that she had barely tasted it. Champagne was famous for being something you could drink all night with no ill effect.

No, it had to be the slivovitz.

A hollow groan from the head of the queue told her that she was not alone in her misery. They'd been knocking back the slivovitz, too.

She ought to open her eyes . . . she ought to try to pass an encouraging word to the others . . . she ought to . . .

Never again. Never slivovitz. Her precarious grip on the world dipped and slipped away. Her head still ached, her stomach still protested, but she slept.

When she woke again later, there was only one consolation. At least the sun hadn't come out. It was a nice grey gloomy day. Thank heaven. Bright, blinding sun would have been more than one could have stood.

The world still had a nasty tendency to begin spinning if she moved her head, but somewhere deep within her some atom of raving optimism insinuated that she might possibly begin to feel human again . . . some day. She wasn't sure she believed it.

'What time is it?' a disembodied voice asked.

A series of groans suggested that people had instinctively moved too quickly to check their watches and were now regretting their helpfulness.

With an effort, Dorrie managed to open both eyes. After the intitial shock, she decided her condition was improving. Very gradually.

No point in rushing your fences. She lay motionless, adjusting to the idea of a new day . . . a new year. Unbidden, the first New Year's Resolution formed in her mind: No more slivovitz.

More groans sounded around her and she began to wonder about the state of the other survivors. She turned her head cautiously and saw that Lucy Bone was head and shoulders out of her sleeping-bag, mouth open gasping for air and eyes staring sightlessly upwards, looking like a beached fish.

'Are you all right, dear?' she asked anxiously.

'I think I'm dying,' Lucy Bone said.

'That's all right then.' Dorrie was obscurely comforted. 'You go back to sleep. You'll be right as rain when you wake up again.'

'Never,' Lucy Bone said, but her eyes closed obediently.

Beyond her, Sakim lay brooding, but Dorrie was beginning to suspect that brooding was his natural state. It was, for some of them. And he had certainly drunk less than anyone else last night and this morning. It was almost as though he did not trust himself to relax among strangers. No need to waste sympathy on that one.

A deep heart-rending groan wrenched her head about too sharply and she groaned herself. When she opened her eyes again, she found Zoltan regarding her with an expression close to sympathy.

'We should never have touched that arak,' he said. 'It is not a Chrr-rristian drink!'

'Do you people realize it's nearly noon?' The voice rose from the head of the queue with querulous incredulity.

'That's all right,' Dorrie comforted. 'We're not going anywhere.'

'Speak for yourself,' Tim Moore said. 'Faye and I have been debating whether to kill ourselves or try for a hair of the dog that bit us.'

'But which dog?' Tony Adair joined the conversation. He had got as far as propping himself up on one elbow, Dorrie noted approvingly, but the effort had turned him a delicate shade of green. 'I feel as though I've been savaged by a pack of mongrels!'

'That arak—' Zoltan said darkly. 'It is not fit for man or beast.'

Talk about the pot calling the kettle black! Dorrie bit down on her personal opinion of slivovitz. Fortunately, Sakim did not appear to be paying attention to Zoltan's mutterings. Just as well, they were all stuck in this queue for another two and a half days. If they began quarrelling among themselves, the atmosphere didn't bear thinking about. It was none too good as it was.

'Oooh . . .' Lucy Bone's eyes opened again. She stared despairingly into space. 'I want to go to the loo, but I'm not sure that I can make it.'

Dorrie became aware that this was also a pressing need of her own. She began to wriggle free of her sleeping-bag.

'Of course you can, dear,' she encouraged. 'It's only across the street.' Her head spun dizzily as she sat up. 'Come on, I'll come with you. If we lean on each other, we ought to be able to stagger over.'

'Wait for me,' Faye said plaintively. 'I'm coming, too. I could never get that far on my own.'

'Come on, then,' Dorrie said. 'If we all stick together, we can make it. And we'll feel ever so much better after a nice wash and brush-up.'

It had been so warm and comfortable in the Powder Room that they had lingered as long as was decently possible. They took an especially long time sitting before the softly lit mirrors, trying to repair the ravages reflected

back at them. Even with the flattering rose-tinted glow of
the boudoir lamps, they winced at the sight.

'Never mind.' Dorrie tried to comfort herself as much
as them. 'It's New Year's Day. What can you expect?'

'Better than this,' Faye muttered, opening her cosmetic
kit and setting to work.

Lucy Bone tried to tug the comb through her tangled
curls by brute force, half-whimpering with the effort. She
seemed the most fragile of them all. Of course she'd
drunk the most arak, what with it being supplied by her
boy-friend.

'You'll never do it that way, dear.' Dorrie took the
comb away from her. 'Here, let me.'

Lucy collapsed forward on to the dressing-table, allowing Dorrie to work gently at the snarled hair. Only a faint
complaining sporadic whimper proved that she had not
entirely lost consciousness.

'We ought to get something to eat before we go back,'
Dorrie said. 'Why don't we stop off in the hotel Coffee
Shop and have a little something? It would help no end.'

'No! Please!'

'I couldn't!'

She was not entirely sorry to be shouted down. She
wasn't sure that she could have eaten anything herself,
but she had at least tried to set a good example. It might
not have been so bad if they could have gone in and had
something simple just set down before them, but the idea
of facing a menu full of strange and exotic dishes was too
much to be contemplated. Even the simplest English
dishes, like kippers or poached eggs, were not to be
thought of right now. Not safely.

'I might be able to manage some black coffee,' Faye admitted carefully. 'But not in the Coffee Shop. There'd be
other people there—eating. I couldn't stand the sight of
food . . .' She shuddered. 'Or the smell.'

'Quite right, dear.' Dorrie gave a sympathetic shudder

of her own, 'Enough is enough, I always say. When we get back to the queue perhaps one of the gentlemen would be kind enough to pop round to a lunch counter and get some coffee for us all. Perhaps that Mr Zoltan will oblige. After all,' she added bitterly, 'It was *his* slivovitz.'

There was a faint moan from the other girl. Dorrie looked at her with some concern. Lucy was dabbing at her temples with a cool damp towel.

'Aren't you any better, dear?'

'No,' Lucy said. 'I'm still dying.'

'Do you think some aspirin might help?' Dorrie rummaged in her handbag. She was sure she had a packet of aspirins in there somewhere.

'No, please. I couldn't choke them down. I just want to go back to sleep. I'll be all right later . . . I suppose.'

'That sounds like a good idea.' Faye pushed herself to her feet and swayed unsteadily for a moment. 'All I want to do is lie down, as well.'

'Sleep's the best medicine.' Dorrie shepherded her charges out of the opulent room and up the plushly-carpeted marble staircase. The sheer luxury of the St Edmund's always had a soothing effect on her, but the girls had obviously had a much softer life than hers and were unimpressed. It was a bit sad, really. She wouldn't recommend it as a long-term thing, but a touch of hardship in early life did make one more appreciative of minor blessings and privileges later on.

She nodded regally to the doorman on the way out. No use pretending they hadn't been in there using the facilities, might as well put the best face on it. He nodded back resignedly and watched their progress across the street.

The queue, she saw as they approached it, had been roused to something approaching animation. They were clustered at the entrance doors and Dorrie felt a momentary qualm. Had there been an accident?

She quickened her steps and the others matched her pace, sensing the faint panic.

Tony Adair stepped aside to let them see what all the fuss was about. A small table had been set up just outside the entrance and covered with a pristine linen cloth. A silver-plated coffee service and china cups and saucers were set out on it. A tray of assorted sandwiches was flanked by a pair of tazza holding an assortment of dainty petit-fours.

'Compliments of Bonnard's,' Tony Adair told them 'And a Happy New Year. Sporting of them, isn't it?'

'Gracious!' Dorrie said. 'They've never done anything like this before.'

'They've never had a hundredth birthday before, either,' Tim Moore laughed.

And they'd never had a Bonnard sleeping in the queue before. Lucy Bone's mouth quirked. What a lot of panic-stricken soul-searching must have been going on. As her friend Dorrie would undoubtedly have said, had she but known, the cat was among the pigeons now, all right.

'We're having black coffee.' Tim was presiding over the coffee-pot. 'What would you girls like?'

'I'll have a drop of cream in mine,' Dorrie decided happily.

'Sure you wouldn't rather have a drop of slivovitz in it?' Tim teased, handing her the cup.

'Or arak,' Zoltan said, refuting the implied slur on his national drink.

'No, thank you!' Dorrie sipped the coffee, it was hot and delicious. Just what they all needed. And she could probably manage a nibble or two of those sandwiches, they were so tiny and they looked so nice, all the crusts neatly trimmed off. Just delicate little triangles filled with succulent pink beef and white turkey, egg mayonnaise, ham, and even plain cream cheese for stomachs that might still be feeling a bit fragile.

'Too bad you missed it,' Tony said 'We had a great chat with the Bonnard's people while they were setting up the table They're a very friendly crew.'

'I can't get over it,' Dorrie said. 'Isn't it lovely of them? So thoughtful, taking all this trouble for us.'

'You're in a Bonnard's queue,' Lucy said. 'Bonnard's look after their own.'

'And quite right, too.' Dorrie glanced at her sharply. There had been something unsettling about the girl's tone. 'Don't speak against it. It's a very good trait to have.'

'I wouldn't know,' Lucy said. 'I haven't run into it very often.'

'Your family —' Dorrie began.

'I have no family,' Lucy Bone said.

'Oh, I'm sorry.' Dorrie was beginning to get a bit annoyed about always being put in the wrong. 'I knew your mother was dead, but I'd thought that your father —'

'He's gone too,' Lucy said shortly. She accepted the coffee unwillingly as it was passed to her. Only the fact that she needed it desperately kept her from pouring it out on the pavement. That, and the fact that she didn't wish to cause a scene right now. It was too early to tip her hand.

Lucy carried the coffee back to her sleeping-bag, uncomfortably aware that Dorrie was following along behind her. She gulped the coffee down and began the familiar retreat into the depths of her sleeping-bag.

'How sad for you,' Dorrie said. 'Losing both your parents. Were they in an accident?'

'No . . .' Lucy tried not to show her impatience. 'My mother died of a sudden virulent infection when I was a child. Soon after that —' her voice choked — 'my father took to chasing after young women.'

'Oh dear,' Dorrie sighed. 'They often do, but you've got

to make allowances. After all, I suppose he was still a young man and—'

'Not all that young,' Lucy said. 'Old enough to know better. It was a pity he didn't.'

'Oh dear,' Dorrie said again. She was going to be glad when this disturbing girl vanished back into her sleeping-bag. 'You mean—?'

'That's right,' Lucy said with finality. 'In the end, it turned out to be the death of him.'

CHAPTER 9

'The mink coat?' Lucien Bonnard's voice rose in outrage. 'But she's *got* a mink coat!'

There were several possible answers to that, but Maggie decided not to try any of them. It would be wiser — and safer — to let the storm blow itself out.

'What is she *doing*?' Lucien asked the impassive ceiling. 'What does she think she's playing at? How long does she imagine this charade can go on? How can — ?'

Maggie leaned back and lit a cigarette as he ranted on. There were times when cancer seemed a lesser evil than a lifetime's involvement with the Bonnard family. What had ever made her think she was strong enough to cope with it? She began silently asking a few questions of her own. How had she become cast as the Wicked Stepmother? She'd only ever met the neurotic brat once. She had hardly begun to know Lucien when his maniac daughter had decamped into an alternative world of God-knew-what: squatting, dissension, drugs, anarchy, you-name-it. As long as it was guaranteed to send a parent into a seizure, the kids were going to dive into it, surfacing only to thumb their noses now and then.

Like now. Maggie took a deep breath, closed her eyes and waited for her ears to tell her when Lucien was running out of steam. Because there was still something else he had to know.

'You don't suppose —'

The change in his voice snapped her eyes open abruptly. She sat forward, watching him intently

'There was an incident a few years ago,' he said slowly. 'At another store. A woman queued for days to buy a mink coat. And then, when she got it, she set fire to it. Burned it in front of all the Fleet Street journalists and photographers. It was some sort of protest about animals.

'You don't suppose — ' His eyes met hers with dawning horror. 'You don't suppose Lucinda has taken up animal welfare? She isn't going to make Bonnard's the laughing-stock of London by wantonly destroying one of the world's most expensive and exclusive mink creations?'

'I don't think you have to worry about that,' Maggie said carefully. 'It isn't very likely that she'll get it, in the first place. You see, she's in second place behind another customer who's queuing for the very same mink coat.'

Lucy Bone had disappeared into her sleeping-bag and was showing no immediate sign of surfacing again.

Dorrie found her charitable instincts sinking to their lowest ebb. It was, she thought, like sitting next to a not very tame tortoise during the hibernation season. Dull, boring and anti-social. What did these people want to join a queue for if they weren't prepared for a little friendly communication? It was all very unsatisfactory.

It was too bad that nice English boy queuing for the cine-camera hadn't joined the queue earlier. It would be a pleasure to have him next to you. Always smiling and friendly, no side to him at all. And those friends of his, coming and going, would have livened things up no end, if only you could hear what they were saying to each other.

No, Dorrie sighed to herself, this was not going to be one of her happiest memories. A shame, because it had boded so well when she had first heard that George and Sandra had their hearts set on an item in the Bonnard's Sale.

Unconsciously Dorrie sighed louder. Her gaze wandered across the intervening spaces and met that of Tony Adair.

'Yes.' He grimaced with sympathy. 'We *are* stuck with a

couple of Sleeping Beauties, aren't we?'

'I wouldn't call them beauties,' Dorrie said.

'Mine isn't, certainly,' Tony Adair agreed. 'But I wouldn't say you had any cause for complaint. Except,' he added judiciously, 'that she doesn't seem to be the friendly sort.'

'I don't think that's entirely her fault.' Dorrie allowed her gaze to sweep over the recumbent Sakim. 'I think she has her problems.'

'Oh?' His own gaze rested thoughtfully on the sleeping form immediately in front of him. 'I hadn't thought of it before, but I dare say you're right.'

'Yes.' Dorrie held his eyes briefly before looking away. It was definitely too bad that so much space separated them. They couldn't have a really good conversation shouting back and forth to each other.

'Mmm,' he said. 'That's rather a shame. I have the feeling that she'd photograph beautifully.'

'Then that will take care of that.' Lucien Bonnard's initial reaction was relief. Maggie waited quietly for the realization of the extent of the problem to catch up with him.

'But —' Unprecedented visions of horror rose behind his eyes: Lucinda in a tug-of-war with a legitimate customer over the mink coat. The scandal! The publicity! Which was just what she wanted, of course.

With a groan, he covered his eyes with his hands, but the visions went on, punctuated by the flaring of flashbulbs as picture after picture was being taken to spread across the front pages of every newspaper in the world.

'The Press . . .' he said. 'If they get hold of this, Bonnard's will be an international laughing-stock. The pictures . . . the headlines . . .'

'I've thought of a few good ones myself,' Maggie said

heartlessly. 'How about: TAKE BACK YOUR MINK. *Bonnard Heiress Battles Customer for Best Buy in Sale . . .?* Or: ALL IN THE FAMILY. *"It's Mine!" Cries Bonnard Heiress as Customer Tries for Bargain Mink . . .?*'

'This is insupportable!' Lucien raised his head, back in a fighting mood again—as she had intended. 'What are we to do?'

'At least the Press haven't got hold of it yet,' Maggie said encouragingly. 'Unless she's planning to tip them off just before the doors open. They could catch the race to the Fur Department then. Should make some smashing action photos.'

'She shouldn't be in the queue at all.' Lucien went back to his main thesis. 'She's a Bonnard. She shouldn't be competing with the customers. She can have anything in the store she wants, just for the asking.'

'She'd have to ask *you*,' Maggie pointed out softly. That was the crux of the whole matter.

'Even then . . .' Lucien was not going to face that yet. 'Even if she fights a customer and wins. Even then, she might still burn the coat.' He shuddered. 'Right in front of a customer who actually *wanted* it!'

'I don't know your daughter too well, Lucien,' Maggie said carefully. 'We only met briefly, and that was a couple of years ago. But I'd say she was perfectly capable of even that.'

'The others in the queue—' Lucien was struck by a new fear. 'Do they know who she is?'

'I don't think so. Foster chatted them up while he was setting out the table. It seems she told them her name was Lucy Bone.'

'That's something, at least.' Lucien shook his head. 'But how long will she keep quiet? I suppose it's too much to hope that she might be a legitimate customer? She simply decided she wanted that coat and didn't want to ask me for it, and so she joined the queue with the others . . .' His voice trailed off. He already knew the answer.

'Even if it were so,' Maggie said. 'It's still going to look terrible. She's one of the Bonnards and she just can't behave like an ordinary citizen. Not when the store is involved. People will automatically put the worst interpretation on it.'

'I know.' Lucien pushed back his chair and walked over to the window. The stone canopy hid the queue from his view, but he stared down intensely none the less. His daughter was down there. And she might as well be hundreds of miles away at some still unknown address. Silent and unreachable, planning to plunge them into scandal. Ready to besmirch the proud name of Bonnard. What did it mean to her? She was already calling herself by some other name. Lucy Bone—ridiculous!

Was there a Mr Bone? There could be, by this time. She had been gone long enough for anything to have happened. Lucien felt a twist of jealousy he refused to acknowledge.

'There'd be no point, I suppose,' Maggie said tentatively, 'in having a little talk with her? Now that you know where she is, Trying to reason with her . . .'

'Do you think she'd listen?' Lucien's face was bleak. 'Do you think she'd even agree to talk to me?'

'It could be arranged,' Maggie said. 'We could invite the entire queue inside for a little cocktail-party. She'd find it hard to refuse if everybody came. And then we could get her away from the rest, into one of the offices, for a private chat.'

'If they keep getting such special treatment,' Lucien said, 'the queue might begin to get suspicious. We've never made such a fuss over them before.'

'There was always the New Year's Eve champagne,' Maggie reflected. 'That set a precedent, of a sort. And this year we have the excuse of the Hundredth Birthday

Celebrations. We mentioned that with the coffee and sandwiches and they accepted it as perfectly natural. Bonnard's is expected to do things in style.'

'Yes,' Lucien agreed thoughtfully. 'Even my darling daughter is determined to bring Bonnard's down in style. She wouldn't admit to queuing for anything less than the special mink.'

'Anyway —' Maggie was encouraged by the first glint of humour he had shown since the situation had developed — 'the Celebrations will give us an out later. It won't establish a dangerous or expensive precedent for coddling the Sales queues if we only do it once every hundred years.'

CHAPTER 10

'Look! Just look!' Dorrie's muted cry of excitement alerted the queue.

They watched the limousine draw up in front of the St Edmund's, the doorman dash down and open the door, saluting, the famous couple step out, self-assured, glowing, and yet somehow diminished, as though one were viewing them through the wrong end of a telescope.

'Brick Ronson and Belva Barrie,' Dorrie sighed happily. 'They're over to make their new film here. *Everyone* stays at the St Edmund's.'

'How funny,' Lucy said. 'They seem so different. They're a lot smaller than I thought they were.'

'It's always that way with film and theatre people, dear,' Dorrie assured her. 'They're always smaller than you think they are. And the men usually have terrible complexions. It's all that make-up they have to wear. Strange, isn't it? Make-up seems to protect a woman's skin, but it's hell on a man's. It just goes to show, it's not really natural for them to wear it. But they have to do it for their Art, poor things.'

'What a lot of luggage,' Faye said, not without admiration. 'Do you suppose they left anything at home at all?'

'I wouldn't have liked to be behind them going through Customs,' Tim said. They watched the hotel minions dealing with the mounds of suitcases. 'They must have a couple of suites to hold all that.'

'One suite, more likely.' Dorrie was knowledgeable on the subject. 'They've been living-in friends for years now.'

They watched the famous couple cross the pavement and go up the steps to the entrance, where they paused and looked back over their shoulders. Seeing the queue, they turned in unison, beaming and bracing themselves. It seemed to disconcert them when the queue did not rush across the street to mob them.

Brick and Belva waved encouragingly, seeming puzzled when the queue, although waving back enthusiastically, remained where they were. It was obviously not the kind of behaviour they were accustomed to, but they appeared to attribute it to the well-known British reserve. Belva's smile widened, Brick waved more warmly. Still they remained unmobbed.

The doorman advanced and murmured something to them; the encouraging expressions faded from their faces. Brick Ronson turned abruptly and entered the hotel. Belva Barric beamed a small shrug across the street, sharing her amusement with the queue and blew a kiss to them before turning to follow him. Either she could take a joke against herself or she had a better sense of Public Relations.

'Americans don't really understand about queues,' Dorrie explained to the others. 'Most of them. They don't have them over there. The only ones who really know about queues are the ones who were here the first year of the Laker Skytrain.' She sighed nostalgically. 'Now *there* was a real queue!'

'You were in that one, were you?' Tony Adair asked with interest. 'That must have been quite an experience.'

'Bless you, it was,' She sighed again. 'I really enjoyed that queue. Such lovely people.'

'You have been to America, then?' Zoltan regarded her with new interest. 'I have often thought —'

'Oh no!' Dorrie said. 'I've never been. It was just,' she explained to the confused expression on their faces, 'that I read in the papers about that queue, and how all those poor people were going to have to wait for three or four days for their seats on a flight home, and I thought what a shame it was when they wanted to be out sightseeing instead of sitting for days in a queue. So I went along and kept places in the queue for a few of them so that they could get out and about and not have their holiday ruined entirely.'

'That was very good of you.'

'Oh, I enjoyed it. I met ever so many nice people and I can't tell you the number of invitations I got to go and visit them in America. I do believe I could go from coast to coast over there and not stay at hotels once.'

'Then why have you not gone?'

'Oh, well.' Dorrie said, flustered. The activity across the street at the St Edmund's had ceased and the queue had now transferred its attention to her and was listening raptly to her interrogation.

'Well, it still takes a lot of money. I know it's cheaper than it used to be, but there's still the transport, and you'd want to bring presents for everybody — you couldn't just pitch up on their doorstep empty-handed to stay with them. And it all mounts up. I've worked it out and I've started saving up, and I buy nice little bits and pieces I find in the Sales after I've got what I'm queuing for. Perhaps I'll manage it some day before I'm too old to enjoy it.'

'You are too generous, I think.' Zoltan nodded, pronouncing his verdict. 'With your time and with your money. You should not worry so much about other people.'

'Well, really!' It was all right for him to talk. Easy enough to see he'd never worried about anybody else in his whole life. But what kind of a world would it be if everyone were like him?'

'You should go, you know,' Lucy Bone said. 'You'd have a wonderful time. It's so —'

'*You* have been?' Zoltan shifted his intent gaze to her. She shrank under it.

'Oh no.' Denial seemed easiest. 'No, I've never been out of the country.' Was that believable? 'Except for school

trips to the Continent,' she added hastily.

They were all looking at her now. She should never have joined in the conversation. Once she started talking, more was apt to slip out than one intended. Sakim had warned her about that. She daren't turn to look at him, it was enough that she could sense his suppressed fury seething behind her.

'Why do you not go?' Zoltan demanded. 'If you have enough money for the mink coat, then you have enough to fly to America for a holiday. It is off-season now, you would still be in time to see all the holiday decorations in New York—they are much more sensational than here. So why do you sit in this dreary queue? Why do you not take the money and fly?

Well! Dorrie thought. *Don't tell me his conscience is bothering him!* He knows he oughtn't to take the mink coat when a nice young girl truly wants it for herself and all he wants is to resell it for a nasty little profit. Perhaps he'll give in if she sticks it out to the bitter end in the queue. And he's afraid he will himself, that's why he's trying to get rid of her. Perhaps there's hope for him yet.

But his words had a strange effect on Lucy Bone. She lost colour and slipped down into the turtleshell of her sleeping-bag. Even Zoltan seemed amazed at her reaction.

He could not know that his words had reminded her of that old telegram traditionally sent to guilty parties: *Fly at once—all is discovered!*

Maggie crossed to the window to see what Lucien was watching so intently. She was just in time to catch Belva Barrie's last laughing wave to the queue.

'Very nice,' Maggie said. 'I expect she'll be over here for her shopping spree as soon as the store opens in the morning?'

'She always is,' Lucien agreed. 'All of them come to Bonnard's. That's often why they stay at the St Edmund's, it's so much more convenient for them They can dip over here in the time they have free between interviews and filming, or whatever they're visiting the country for.'

'And no worrying about waiting for the Sale to start for them,' Maggie said. 'Nothing but the best and the price is no object.' She laughed shortly.

'What's so funny?'

'I just had a sudden thought.' Maggie abruptly became aware that it might not sound so amusing to Lucien. 'I — I just thought, suppose *she* falls for the floor-length mink, too? Wouldn't that be something? To have *her* lined up in the queue with the others?'

'Very droll.' Lucien turned away impatiently and stalked back to his desk.

Maggie sighed. All right, so it wasn't that funny, but Lucien was letting this get to him too much. It was destroying his sense of humour, overshadowing their relationship.

Which was precisely what Lucinda Bonnard wanted.

For that reason alone, it could not be allowed to. Maggie prowled after Lucien, stepping as delicately as a cat. He gave no indication that he was aware that she remained in the room.

'I'll say one thing.' Still she tried for the light touch. 'You do see life here at Bonnard's. And isn't there some Middle-Eastern potentate arriving at the St Edmund's any time now? I suppose we'll get the harem in here doing their shoplifting.'

'The Sheikh is one of our most valued customers!' Lucien snapped out of the lethargy he had been drifting into, a merchandising gleam appeared in his eye. 'He hasn't been here for some time. All the trouble in his territory has kept him close to home over the past few years. I look forward to welcoming him to Bonnard's again. And his entourage.' He frowned briefly. 'Your suggestion that any of them might indulge in shoplifting is, of course, ridiculous. The Sheikh is an honourable man and the penalty he would exact from any one of his people—'

'You mean, "Off with their hands"?' Maggie asked uncertainly. Could Lucien be joking?

'Exactly,' Lucien said. 'I can assure you we never have trouble from any of *his* subjects.'

'He sounds a real charmer,' Maggie said weakly. Her stomach seemed to have just done a loop-the-loop.

'He is.' Lucien was unaware of irony. 'Just wait until you meet him. And wait until you see him in action. It's shopping on the grand scale. You may think you've seen something with some of the other Middle-Easterners we've had in here, but . . .' He shrugged dismissively. 'Nothing! Compared to the Sheikh. There's been nothing like him since the old-style Maharajahs at the turn of the century.'

'I can hardly wait,' Maggie said. 'Racks full of *haute couture* and floors full of furniture, eh? Perhaps we ought to alert the Shipping Department to stand by for action.'

'They're already prepared,' Lucien answered absently, reminding her afresh, although he probably hadn't intended it that way, that Bonnard's was a long-established institution, with no need of Johnny-come-latelys to teach them how to conduct their business.

'I should have known.' Maggie's voice was subdued. Bonnard's had been smoothly and efficiently functioning for a century before she had come along. If she were to die tomorrow, it would go on without so much as a ripple on the surface to mark her passing.

'Maggie?' Lucien became aware of her mood suddenly. He stretched out his hand and drew her to him. 'Maggie, you've got a lot to learn about Bonnard's—the store and the family. But, please—' his arms tightened around her—'please don't let anything you learn discourage you. We're all depending on you now. More than you may ever know.'

Three children, Maggie decided, nestling against him, Three was a good number and the sex didn't matter. Three would ensure that the Bonnard line was safely carried on for generations yet.

And three would keep Lucien so preoccupied that he might forget the disappointment Lucinda had been to him.

CHAPTER 11

They had all been half dozing through the long som-
nolent afternoon. The earlier greyness had turned into a
steady dull rain which discouraged any thoughts of leaving their comfortable, carefully-constructed little snugs of
blankets and cushions and roaming away from the queue.
Heads had stopped throbbing and stomachs had settled
down. Among the more ambitious, there was even the
hope that energy might return by tomorrow morning—or
at least the morning after that when the Sale started.

Behind them, Bonnard's display windows glowed
brightly, providing enough light to read the newspapers
they had bought from an enterprising newsvendor who
had walked slowly past the queue, in rather the manner
that taxis slowed as they passed long bus queues. The
news thus obtained was enough to provide a mildly
interesting reading session, but not of sufficient portent to
jolt them into full wakefulness.

Another degree of darkness shaded over the city and
the street lamps switched on. The large golden globes
flanking the entrance to the St Edmund's sprang into life,
glowing discreetly with a soft diffused radiance that
meant one could look directly into them without blinking.

The world began to seem a warmer, more cheerful
place.

'These film people—' Even Zoltan seemed to feel it. He
ventured what was practically his first civil word since his
advice to Lucy Bone had been rebuffed earlier in the day.
'On page 5, there is a photograph of them arriving at the
airport this morning.' He frowned at it judiciously. 'I
think she is prettier in real life.'

There was a flurry of turning pages as the others hurried to respond to his overture.

'Probably exhausted, poor dear, getting off the plane at that hour of the morning,' Dorrie said. 'And with having just gone through Customs.'

'She photographs like a dream,' Tony Adair judged professionally. 'It's just that everything looks better in colour. Just look at that bone structure!'

Sakim glared at Tony, although it had seemed a perfectly innocent remark. Lucy raised a hand absently to brush her own cheekbone. 'I suppose that's a colour camera you're after?' she asked.

'Good Lord, yes!' Tony turned to look fondly over his shoulder at the displayed cine-camera. He did this anyway, so frequently that one might suspect he feared someone was going to discover that a mistake had been made and rush into the show window at the last minute to remove it from the sale.

They all harboured this secret nightmare, Dorrie had decided a long time ago. Certainly, she even felt twinges of it herself, especially when she was queuing for something someone else wanted desperately. Which brought her recent thoughts round full circle again. It was a shame that poor little Lucy was waiting so patiently in the queue and yet hadn't a hope of getting her heart's desire.

Dorrie had tried to divert her to some more accessible fur. As one would with a child, she had pointed out the lustrous gloss of the chinchilla stole, the artful drape of a sable cape, praising them in the hope that they would stir a spark of acquisitiveness. But the child had just smiled wanly and bravely, refusing to give up on her original choice.

Worse, Zoltan had begun listening with more interest than was comfortable. He needn't think he was going to walk off with all the furs in the Sale! It shouldn't be allowed—it probably wasn't. But somebody ought to do something about that one. He was sharp enought to cut himself—after which, being the sort he was, he'd undoubtedly bleed messily over everyone else in sight.

A word appeared mistily at the back of Dorrie's mind and she struggled to force it away from her consciousness. It was not a particularly nice word, but it was one the late Mr Witson had been in the habit of using frequently. More in connection with horse races than with the human race, but the principle was the same.

The word was: *nobbled.*

Sakim was growing excessively tiresome. Once Lucy Bone had admitted the thought, it would not go away.

How could it when, every moment, Sakim was proving the truth of it?

Not content with bobbing his head into her line of vision every time she tried to speak to Tony Adair, he had now started a low growling obligato to the conversation Tony was trying to carry on with her. The fact that whatever Sakim was saying was in his own native language did not matter, the implications were coming over loud and clear. In another few minutes, he'd be making a scene.

Really, it was very kind of Tony Adair to continue trying to talk to her at all under the circumstances. And, let Sakim growl as much as he liked, she had no intention of being intimidated into silence. She was not one of his downtrodden countrywomen, she was English.

Ironically enough, in the beginning, he had claimed that he liked her because she had a mind and a will of her own. It was increasingly noticeable lately, however, that whenever she tried to use either of these qualities, they infuriated him.

'. . . and then, for the finale . . .' Tony swung forward, trying to maintain eye contact around the implacable barrier of Sakim's back.

'Yes?' She leaned outwards to meet him. Sakim's glower increased.

'Well, we—'

Sakim stood up abruptly. 'We go get something to eat now,' he announced.

'I don't want anything,' Lucy said. 'But you go ahead.'

This was obviously unsatisfactory. Sakim sat down again. His fury mounted visibly.

'Go along, old man, if you're hungry,' Tony said amiably. 'Don't worry. I'll keep your place for you.'

'That was not what Sakim was worrying about. He turned and glared at Tony, then swung back to glare at Lucy.

If looks could kill . . . Dorrie thought uneasily.

'He should be careful, that young man,' Zoltan said softly at her shoulder. 'He will wind up with a knife between his ribs. These people are very jealous of their women.'

'Oh, it would never come to that.' Dorrie spoke as much to protest her own thoughts as his.

'You think not?' Zoltan smiled disbelievingly. 'I have lived in the East. I have seen such things—' He seemed to notice that he was causing distress. Dorrie was shaking her head in negation, Faye and Tim were listening with horror.

'Perhaps you are right,' he conceded. 'Perhaps he will only beat up the girl to teach her her place.'

This caused even more distress.

'Oh no!' Faye cried, appalled.

'He can't do that—she's English,' Tim said comfortingly.

'Ah, but *he* is not,' Zoltan pointed out. He looked at their stricken faces and shrugged. 'Whatever happens,' he said, 'we can only hope that it does not happen here. We do not want to be involved.'

'Dorrie! Auntie Dorrie!' The children, running ahead of their mother, engulfed her abruptly. She had been so caught up in the conversation that she had not noticed them approaching.

'We brought your tea,' Carol announced proudly: her brother, Ron, nodded shy agreement.

'Did you then? Wasn't that kind of you?' She smiled at Sandra, who had now joined them, her carrier bag bulging.

'I made a nice thick beef stew,' Sandra said, beginning to unpack. She gave Dorrie a wide-mouthed vacuum flask. 'Hot and hearty. And fresh tea—'

'And rock cakes,' Carol reminded. 'Lots and lots of rock cakes.'

'Lots?' Dorrie played along obligingly. 'Shall we have one now, then!'

'They're for you.' Sandra frowned at her daughter. 'We have plenty more at home for ourselves.'

Dorrie decided to let the matter drop. Young Sandra had her own ideas about child-raising and didn't thank you for going against them.

'A few sandwich rolls—' Sandra passed over a parcel. 'I made fresh rolls, they've cheese-and-chutney filling.'

'Lovely!' Dorrie began transferring the items into her holdall. She wasn't really hungry right now, but she would be later.

'And a new book.' Sandra displayed a crisp volume, its cover depicting a small tent set up on some Arctic waste, icebergs towering in the background. 'The librarian said you'd like it. It's just come in, so she knows you haven't read it.'

'Ooh, lovely. I've just finished this one.' Dorrie brought out the mountaineering adventure she had been reading. 'If you'll return it for me and thank her very much—'

'Glad to,' Sandra said. 'Now, is there anything else you'd like? Any errands that need doing?'

'No, I think—' Dorrie stopped. 'Well, if you wouldn't mind,' she said. 'Just stay here in the queue for a minute while I pop across the street . . .'

'Your friend is a very nice lady, I think,' Zoltan said, as they watched Dorrie cross the street and go up the steps of the St Edmund's.

'You don't know how nice,' Sandra said. 'She's always doing something for other people. Like waiting all this time in the queue for us. George and I could never have managed it on our own, and we know we'd never find a fridge-freezer at such a bargain again. It will make all the difference to us when we go into the pub.'

'Your friend seems to enjoy queues. They are, I think, almost a hobby for her.'

'I suppose that's really what they are,' Sandra agreed thoughtfully. 'I used to think she liked them because they reminded her of the war.'

'Ah yes, your finest hour.'

'You needn't say it like that,' Sandra said. 'I don't even remember it. But, if other people want to, I don't see why they shouldn't.'

'I did not mean —' He broke off with a puzzled frown, obviously wondering why the English were so quick to take umbrage at the most innocent remark.

'She must be a lovely neighbour.' Faye leaned forward and spoke around Zoltan.

'Oh, she is,' Sandra said. 'She really makes all the difference. I mean, we live in a tower block — and you know the way people are always complaining about them. But ours isn't like that at all. We all know each other and help each other. But, really, Auntie Dorrie helps more than anyone else, and she's mostly the reason we all know each other. Because she talks to us all and tells us who she's queuing for and what they want, and then it's only natural to chat to them when we see them and ask them if they're enjoying their bargain.'

'She is a focal point.' Zoltan nodded. 'I can understand how this could happen. As you say, it makes all the difference.'

'Oh, it does. The rest of the estate knows her, too, and knows she lives in our block, and so people stop us to ask us about her and how she is. There have even been stories in the local newspaper about her, with pictures of her visiting some of her friends and standing beside the things she's queued to get for them. She's quite famous where we live.'

'Mum—' Ron nudged his mother imploringly. 'Mum, do you think she'd get something for me?'

'Well, you'd have to ask her, wouldn't you?' Momentarily diverted, her suspicions aroused, she added sharply, 'What is it you want?'

'I've got enough money to pay.' He evaded the direct question. 'I've saved it up out of my pocket money. Please, Mum.'

'Here comes Auntie Dorrie!' His sister's cry saved him. They watched Dorrie hurrying across the street, waving to the children as she came.

'That was quick.' Sandra greeted her with amusement.

'Yes, well, I knew you were waiting. You have to get back to look after the baby, don't you?'

'I left her next door,' Sandra said. 'She'll be well cared for until I get back. There's no rush. I thought I might look in at a couple of the stores, while I'm here.'

'That's a good idea, dear.' Dorrie glanced around at the others who, having nothing better to do, were a moderately rapt audience. 'Why don't I just walk you down to the corner, then? I could do with a bit of exercise.'

One of the children on each side of her, clinging to her hands, she walked with Sandra beyond earshot of the queue. As they reached the corner, she freed herself and took out the note she had hastily scribbled in the St Edmund's.

I wonder, dear, if you'd mind just picking up a couple of little things for me?' She gave the note to Sandra. 'You can get the odd sounding one at the chemist's.'

'You're all right?' Sandra asked quickly.

'Bless you, yes. It's nothing, really. Just something I happened to remember from my childhood. There's no problem, it won't be on prescription. But you might have to go to two or three chemists before you find it. Try the really old-fashioned chemists first. There probably isn't much call for it these days.'

'Never heard of it myself,' Sandra said cheerfully, running her eye over the shopping-list. 'There'll be no problem about the cherry brandy, though. No — and you can put that away!' She pushed aside the money Dorrie was offering. 'As though we'd let you pay for anything, after all you're doing for us.'

'Oh, but —'

'I wouldn't hear of it. And George would be furious with me if I did!' Sandra turned away resolutely.

'But I wanted it to be *my* treat. They're *my* friends in the queue.'

'Yes, and no wonder they're so fond of you. That man with the accent just ahead of you is a great admirer of yours.'

'Oh dear, is he?' Dorrie was stricken with guilt. She stretched out a hand, as though to stop Sandra, but the lights had changed and Sandra was already shepherding the children across the street.

Well, after all, Dorrie soothed her rumbling conscience. Just because you *had* something, it didn't mean you had to *use* it.

CHAPTER 12

The queue was settling down for the night. The first two were snuggled into their sleeping-bags, although the transistor beside Zoltan's camp bed still thrummed softly with a soothing background of orchestral music being transmitted from some Continental station.

Dorrie had been promising herself for some time now that she was just going to read a few more pages and then call it a night herself. But, as the expedition struggled across the frozen Arctic wastes, losing heart and chewing on pieces of dried pemmican, Dorrie poured another cup of tea, fumbled for another rock cake and curled her toes luxuriously against the freshly-filled hot-water bottle which was radiating warmth through her sleeping-bag.

There was nothing like reading about other people's troubles to make you appreciate how comfortable you were. The librarian had been right — it was just the sort of book she liked. In the summer, mind you, queuing for the July Sales, it was cozier to read about desert crossings, sandstorms, parched throats and burning eyes. Then you realized how lucky you were to be sitting comfortably in the shade, with ice tinkling in a Thermos of lemonade and all the comforts of civilization just a few short steps away.

In just another minute she was going to put down the book and go to sleep. Dorrie turned the page: a fissure was opening up in the ice ahead of them and the huskies were heading straight for it, the other members of the expedition not having realized yet that their leader had gone snowblind half an hour ago and was trying to keep it from them. Dorrie nibbled at her rock cake and kept on reading.

Sakim wasn't asleep yet. Although he kept his eyes closed, Lucy could sense his wakefulness — and his fury. He was working himself up into one of the murderous rages that swept over him periodically, reducing his friends to frightened placating shadows of themselves, terrifying her.

This time she didn't care.

He had gone too far. He had, perhaps, been going too far for quite a long while without her noticing it. She had made allowances for cultural differences and excused his rudeness because his command of English was less than that of her friends.

Why should she be the one to make all the concessions? He was the one who had chosen to come to this country. Surely he should adapt to its customs, rather than try to force everyone he came in contact with into his ways?

At first the differences between them had intrigued and amused her. She had been more than willing to listen to the endless stories of his homeland, to try to go along with some of the less restricting customs, to dip her toes into the waters of an alien culture. How was it that she was suddenly in so deep? Was she in over her head?

Not quite. But perhaps her dissatisfaction would not have crystallized so soon if they had been almost totally surrounded by English people. She had not realized that she had been missing them so much.

Nor had she realized that she had missed the company of English men so much. The casual, non-sexual encounters, the light, undemanding conversation. Tony Adair had actually said something — she forgot what — that had made her laugh aloud. Looking back, she tried to remember how long it had been since she had laughed because of something her partner in conversation had said.

Too long. And it was not entirely her fault. She had not been paying attention — that was the worst she could accuse herself of. It was bad enough. Without realizing it, she had allowed herself to be taken over. Socially, as well as emotionally.

How often had Sakim — in the early days before she had moved — answered the telephone in her flat when she had been in another room, muttered something and replaced the receiver? When she'd asked who had called, he had invariably told her it had been a wrong number. She began to wonder about that now — Now that he was behaving so badly about Tony Adair. Sulking like a child because she dared talk to another man. If he couldn't trust her any better than that —

But he didn't. In other ways, perhaps, but not where other men were concerned. At first it had been mildly flattering — when it wasn't blatantly hilarious. The men he had glared at! Men she wouldn't even have glanced at. He had even been jealous of that silly foreigner just in front of Dorrie. It was suddenly clear to her. That was why he had objected to their joining the queue the first time they had arrived.

Sakim had surveyed the short queue, glowered, and announced that they must first walk around the outside of the store and up and down the surrounding streets to make sure that everything was as innocent as it seemed. For nearly an hour they had threaded their way in and out of the intersecting streets for blocks around, looping past the queue intermittently. Each time, he had shaken his head and continued past. Finally, he had announced that they would come back in the morning.

In the morning, they had found Dorrie firmly ensconced in the place behind Zoltan and, seeing this, Sakim had consented to their getting into the queue. He had then positioned her behind Dorrie, in front of himself, effectively cutting her off from contact with any other male. She had the impression that he would have preferred a couple more women between her and Zoltan, but had to

settle for the situation as it was since he could not be sure
that the next person to join the queue would not be
another male and he could not keep her walking around
indefinitely or she would have begun to suspect his real
motive.

He would undoubtedly have preferred women behind
him, too. It was just his bad luck that Tony Adair had
joined the queue — and that Tony was talkative, out-
going, friendly, with an interesting job he was absorbed
in.

All the things she had been missing unconsciously during these past few months.

But she could not let herself consider that. Not when
she was irrevocably committed to her present course of
action. She would rethink her situation later . . . after-
wards . . .

Car doors slammed and there was a sudden commotion at
the end of the queue: clattering, crashing, loud laughter
and louder giggles.

The others, awakened or disturbed just at the point of
dropping off to sleep, stirred, sat up and glared down
towards the source of all the noise.

'Shh!' Someone warned belatedly. There was another
ripple of unrepentant merriment.

'*Now* see what you've done!' One of the women turned
towards the watching faces and shrugged, pantomiming
helplessness. 'I'm *so* sorry. He just won't be quiet!'

'Sorry. Sorry.' One of the men waved to the queue — it
was to be hoped that he was not the one who had been
driving. 'Didn't wake you, I hope? No,' he answered his
own question. 'You couldn't have been sleeping like this.
Catch up on your sleep after the big day, eh?'

'Oh dear,' Dorrie sighed. 'I hope *they're* not planning
to stay awake and be noisy all night!' There was no doubt
about it, Bonnard's merchandise might be as desirable as

ever, but Bonnard's queue left a lot to be desired.

'Actually,' Tony Adair informed the newcomers, 'we *do* sleep at night here. We sleep quite well. Usually.'

Good for him. Dorrie gave an approving nod.

'Who are these people?' Zoltan demanded urgently, quite as though she knew the answers. 'What do they want?'

'I'm afraid they're joining the queue.' Dorrie knew that much. 'You've got to expect it now, you know. There's only one more day before the Sale begins. We'll be getting a lot more people in the queue over the next twenty-four hours.'

He said something in a language she couldn't understand — and just as well probably — and hurled himself pctulantly back into his former position, his camp bed rocking wildly. The impression was strong that he was not pleased. Well, who was?

'You girls sure you want to go through with this?' The words drifted back along the queue. 'The radio forecast snow before morning.'

'Now you stop trying to frighten us,' one of the women trilled. 'We're quite determined.'

"That's right,' the other one chimed in. 'You'll just have to get your own meals tomorrow — and wash your own dishes.' The last was thrown out in a rather hopeless tone, more in the manner of one trying to implant a suggestion than state a fact.

The men whooped with laughter, letting everyone know that humouring the little woman wasn't going to extend *that* far.

'Oh, really!' Lucy had partially emerged from her sleeping-bag and had been watching them, propped up on one elbow. Now she sighed with exasperation and caught Tony Adair's eye.

'Some people are awful,' he murmured softly — and winked. 'While others are bloody awful.'

'I will not be insulted!' Sakim sprang up like a jack-in-the box and whirled on Tony 'Always you laugh at me! You think I do not know? I am not stupid —'

'Then you're giving a good imitation,' Tony said. 'No one was even thinking about you.'

'Sit down!' Lucy tugged at Sakim's trouser leg. 'You're making a scene!'

'A scene? A scene? Oh, you are so English —'

'Well, what do you expect?' Dorrie asked reasonably. 'She *is* English. Don't tell us you never noticed that before.'

'You are all against me!' Sakim accused wildly. 'You all hate me!'

'Not yet,' Tony said, 'but keep working on it. You're making great progress.'

At least it had silenced the newcomers to the queue. They stood watching, then withdrew several yards and huddled together in earnest discussion. It appeared that fresh arguments were being presented as to the wisdom of becoming associated — however briefly — with such a motley and unvouched-for group of strangers.

Random emphasized words drifted back to the queue. '*Fight . . . foreigner . . . unstable . . . dangerous . . .*'

'You see —' Zoltan said censoriously. 'This sort of thing gives the whole queue a bad name.' He turned his head and spoke across Dorrie to Lucy. 'Can you not control your friend?'

'Sakim, sit down!' Lucy said desperately, abandoning all pretence that they were not long-standing friends, that they had just met in the queue. She tugged again at his trouser leg.

Sakim squatted abruptly, muttering to himself.

Tony looked at Lucy and obviously decided against saying anything more. Rather ostentatiously, he lay back and closed his eyes.

Dorrie hoped that he was secretly keeping one eye at least half open. After all, he was right next to Sakim and that strange young man was in a very uncertain mood. She wouldn't trust him as far as she could throw him herself. And if he had caught and understood some of the compliments Tony had been paying to Lucy earlier in the day . . .

Personally she was quite glad that Lucy was between herself and Sakim, although that presented danger, too. She determined that she was going to keep an eye open herself. Suppose he went berserk in the night and decided to attack Lucy? Someone had better keep watch.

Cautiously the newcomers moved back towards the end of the queue. The women appeared to have won the argument. Besides, things had quietened down now. It was perfectly safe. After all, they were right outside Bonnard's — that, in itself, was such a bulwark of respectability that it was impossible to imagine anything untoward happening there. Across the street, the imposing façade of the St Edmund's Hotel loomed comfortingly, reinforcing the promise of safety. One couldn't let oneself be deterred from one's goal by a tempest in a teapot.

But it would be just as well to be careful. The men began erecting a defensive barrier of overnight cases, extra cushions, and equipment immediately behind Tony Adair, thus cutting off their wives from the rest of the queue. If the party started getting rough again, the low barricade might trip or delay possible pursuers long enough to give the women time to get clear.

'I still don't like it, Janice,' one of the men said. 'I wish you'd give up this nonsensical idea and come home.'

'Geoff's right,' the other man agreed. 'You don't need to do this sort of thing — ' His booming laugh fanfared the proclamation to the rest of the queue. 'It isn't as though we kept you short of housekeeping money!'

'It isn't that, Dave.' The woman sent a nervous apologetic smile towards the others. 'Not for anyone. It's just a — '

'A bit of adventure,' the woman called Janice supplied.

'Make sure you don't get more than you bargained for.' The man sent a suspicious look along the queue, but Sakim had settled down, crouching lower, silent now and looking quite harmless.

'We'll be all right.' There was a trace of impatience in her voice. 'You needn't worry.'

'I don't like to leave you here,' Geoff said.

'Then stay here with us.'

'You know we can't do that!' Both men shied back at the idea. 'We have to go to work in the morning.'

'Well, then . . .' The woman shrugged.

In the distance, a church clock chimed the half-hour after midnight.

'It's morning already,' the woman pointed out. 'There's only one more day now.'

'And two nights,' the man said, but it was a losing battle and he was aware of it.

'Anyway, this night's half over, for a start.' While the men stood by, defeated but still reluctant to admit it, the women began settling into their new territory.

Janice took the place immediately behind the make-shift barrier separating them from Tony Adair, the other woman behind her. They did not have sleeping-bags, but set up camp stools and cocooned themselves in blankets.

They would not be particularly comfortable, Dorrie reckoned, but it wouldn't kill them, either. You could tell it was their first time in a long-term queue. Before this, they'd probably never waited more than half an hour at the butcher's.

The men hovered, edging imperceptibly towards the end of the pavement and the waiting car.

'Look,' one of them said. 'If you change your minds . . . get fed up . . . just ring and one of us will come and collect you. Don't be silly about it. We won't tease you for giving up. Just ring. Promise?'

After murmured assurances, the men turned and gratefully escaped. The women watched the car drive away, then turned to survey the queue.

But the queue had retreated into itself. It was too late to be sociable. Morning was time enough to enquire into the new arrivals. By morning, or perhaps mid-morning, it was on the cards that still more people would have joined the queue. Let the newcomers make friends with them. The long-established queue members were already a group on their own, knit together by the long hours spent in each other's company. They knew each other's little ways now and it hardly seemed worthwhile to bother to accommodate themselves to people who were going to be with them for such a short while.

Besides, the newcomers had already cut themselves off by their ridiculous barricade. Dorrie was not surprised to find that she had formed definite allegiances. This was not the best queue she had ever been in, but it could have been worse. It was stupid, as well as insulting, for these new people to behave as though there was something sinister about it. If they felt like that, why had they joined it at all? Why didn't they go back where they came from?

Zoltan raised his head and stared at her. For a moment, she was afraid she had spoken the final thought aloud. There were too many people near her who might take it personally, neither of them the people it was intended for.

'What do they want?' he repeated his earlier question. 'What are they queuing for?'

'We'll find out in the morning, I expect,' Dorrie said comfortably. 'It's a bit late to start a conversation at this hour.'

He nodded, half-asleep but reassured. Even if they were after the furs he had earmarked for his own, they were too late. He was so far ahead of them in the queue that they hadn't a chance. Apart from which, they might be after something quite different. In that case, it was someone else's worry.

Dorrie took an automatic maternal check up and down the queue. Faye and Tim were already back to sleep, Zoltan was dropping off even now. Tony Adair had turned his back—quite properly—on the strangers and huddled down in his sleeping-bag. Sakim was also back in his sleeping-bag, seemingly over his fit of temper. One arm was stretched across the bottom of Lucy's sleeping-bag, his hand lightly probing as though to imprison her ankle again.

It was all very well if you liked that sort of thing, Dorrie supposed, but that constant possessiveness would drive her up the wall. It was surprising Lucy didn't mind it. Perhaps modern young girls weren't so independent as was commonly supposed.

Still, even if the girl didn't mind it now, that wasn't to say she wouldn't find it cloying and infuriating in a few more years. Perhaps not that long. Dorrie looked at the girl's face. Her eyes were closed, but she was frowning. As though in her sleep, she turned on her side, curling up slightly, neatly removing her ankle from the groping hand. With her head safely turned away, she opened her eyes abruptly and caught Dorrie watching her.

Dorrie blushed, hoping it was too dark for it to be noticed, and glanced away quickly. When she looked back, the girl had her eyes closed again and Sakim had retreated completely into his own sleeping-bag. That was all right, then.

Damned old bag! If anything more was needed to fan Lucy's fury, that provided it. *Peeping Thomasina!* Getting second-hand thrills, was she from watching and imagining activities that were beyond her now? She should know—she should really know—the truth of the matter. That would give her something to think about and jolt her out of her complacency.

It wasn't love, desire, or even lust that kept Sakim's hand creeping towards the foot of her sleeping-bag. It was the constant need to reassure himself that the loaded gun was still there, safely hidden away in the secret pocket sewn into the bottom of her sleeping-bag. Waiting for the moment when they would use it.

CHAPTER 13

'It's started snowing,' Lucien said from the window.

'It may not be snowing in London.' Maggie was damned if she was going to get out of the warm bed and join him at the window. The fire was a barely-remembered glow in the fireplace and the chill wind was curling into the bedroom through a thousand chinks, loose-fitting doors, casements, wastepipes, ventilating ducts and God knew what else. Maggie could never understand why the English bothered to open windows. The way they built their houses, they were never very cut off from the Great Outdoors. What did surprise her was that people occasionally managed to commit suicide by gassing themselves to death, having first sealed off all the draughts. That took real determination.

'It probably isn't snowing in London,' she said wistfully. 'It's always warmer in the city.'

'Possibly.' Lucien sounded unconvinced. As she had feared he would, he opened the window and leaned out, squinting up at the sky as though trying to gauge the extent of the storm. An icy wind swirled snowflakes into the room.

'Luu-cien,' Maggie wailed. 'It's freezing in here.'

'Yes, yes.' Lucien drew back into the room, but remained standing by the open window.

'The window,' she said patiently. 'Shut the window, Lucien. You might even,' she added hopefully, 'do something about the fire.'

'Oh, yes.' He moved absently to the fireplace and tossed pieces of wood on to the smouldering ashes, sending up a shower of sparks. It was clear that his mind was not on what he was doing and he had still left the window open.

He sank into the chair beside the fire and poked half-
heartedly at the wood, trying to ignite it without further
effort.

'Lucien!' With a deep sigh, Maggie threw back the
covers and pulled on her robe, shivering as she tied it
around her. She crossed to the window and slammed it
shut, then went over to the fireplace and took the poker
from Lucien's hand, wielding it briskly. A faint growing
glow rewarded her. She added tinder and watched it
catch.

'Lucinda is warm and comfortable in her sleeping-bag.'
Maggie spelled it out for him. 'There's no need to worry
about her. You know where she is and where she'll be for
the next thirty-six hours. We'll get a chance to talk to her
at the "impromptu" cocktail-party tomorrow. Maybe we
can get through to her. If not, at least you'll have tried.'

'And . . . after that?' Lucien voiced the thought upper-
most in his mind. He had made other overtures. Endlessly.
He had not Maggie's optimism about the outcome of this
one.

'Then we'll think of something else,' Maggie said firmly.
'Now come back to bed and stop worrying. *She's* all
right — and giving *me* pneumonia won't solve anything.'

But it would, Maggie realized abruptly. If she were to
die, Lucinda would once again be the sole heiress to the
Bonnard estate, with no step-brothers or sisters looming
on the horizon to challenge her inheritance.

Without her, the threat might never arise again.
Lucien was not a man who loved easily. Not for him the
casual changing of partners to sport a younger, more up-
to-date model on his arm. Lucien loved deeply — and for
keeps. And so did she.

Three children, my darling, she promised silently. She
had already stopped taking the Pill, although she had not
mentioned the fact to Lucien. Nothing had happened
yet, but she hoped . . . soon. Then she could show Lucien

what family life could be like, what it ought to be like — in a happy, united family. Meanwhile, the wedding would go forward as planned — immediately after the Sale — and nothing would stop it.

'All right,' Lucien rose with a sigh. 'You're right, of course. Let's go back to bed.'

Three children, my darling. She nestled in his arms. *And I won't die on you and leave them to be brought up by strangers and turned into strangers to you. There'll be parties and love and laughter. You don't know how happy you're going to be.*

Frost sparkled on the rooftops and glazed the pavement as the morning gradually dawned. Another grey day, but what could you expect at this time of the year?

Dorrie was the first awake, she usually was. She preferred it that way, it gave her time to pull herself together and get settled comfortably for the day before the others began to stir.

Moving quietly, she collected her empty Thermos, lukewarm hot-water bottle and sponge-bag and wriggled out of her sleeping-bag. She'd freshen up, taking her time about it, in the luxurious warmth of the St Edmund's, refill her hot-water bottle and make fresh tea in her Thermos. It occurred to her that the St Edmund's was better value to the Bonnard's January Sale queue than to their July Sale queue. All that gloriously hot, nearly boiling, water constantly on tap wasn't so necessary in July.

Well, just this last day, and then the next time she was in a Bonnard's queue, it would be the July one. Almost certainly. There was always something someone wanted from Bonnard's.

The night porter nodded resignedly to her as she entered. Once past him, Dorrie glanced at her watch. It was just about another half-hour before he went off duty, so she could stay quite a long while if she pleased. The day porter wasn't to know that she hadn't come in just before he went on duty. In any case, he wouldn't much care. The porters were too concerned with their constant flow of celebrities and dignitaries to worry about something so insignificant as the Bonnard's queue. They were simply something to be suffered twice a year and forgotten about the rest of the time.

She was half way across the foyer before she became aware of the following footsteps and a voice hailed her.

'You're an early bird, Dorrie.'

'Look who's talking.' She smiled as Tony Adair came up to her. 'I didn't know you were awake, or I'd have said good morning.'

'I just woke up as you were starting across the street and decided to follow your lead.' He brushed a hand across his blue-shadowed chin. 'Get an early start and make myself presentable.'

'Mmm-hmm.' Dorrie noted the electric shaver not quite concealed in his hand. No prizes for guessing who he wanted to see him at his best. She nodded approvingly. It wasn't a bad idea. There he'd be, all bright-and-shining morning face, while Sakim—there was no denying—looked at his seediest and sleaziest first thing in the morning. Lucy was bound to notice the contrast. It might be a slightly dirty trick, but all was fair in love and war.

'It feels good to get into the warmth, doesn't it?' He was in no hurry to get on with his morning routine. Of course, there was never a chance for a private conversation in the queue with everyone listening.

'I always like to sit down for a bit here in the lobby and thaw out,' Dorrie said, not quite truthfully, but giving him an opening if he wanted to take it. It appeared that he did. He seated himself beside her on the leather sofa opposite the palatial grand staircase leading up to the Salons and down to the Rest Rooms.

'This is a beautiful old building.' He looked around

appreciatively, breathing in the atmosphere. 'They don't make them like this any more.'

'More's the pity,' Dorrie said. 'I always think it's a shame everyone doesn't get the chance to see places like this, then maybe they'd begin to realize what they're missing with all the glass-and-steel boxes they're having foisted on them these days.'

'You feel that way too, do you?' he asked eagerly. 'I've been thinking that I wish I could show it to people. You see,' he confessed, almost shyly, 'I never see a place that's out of the ordinary, either very grand or the opposite, without thinking what a marvellous film set it would make.'

'It would, wouldn't it?' Dorrie looked around with new interest, seeing it through his eyes. 'That staircase now, you could do a lot with that.'

'Real Busby Berkeley stuff,' he agreed. 'And room on it for the full chorus. Practically room enough for the orchestra, too.'

'And all the beautiful colours. They would photograph well, wouldn't they?' She was suddenly anxious, entering into the spirit of the thing.

'Like a dream,' he said. 'Especially with the new cine equipment I'm queuing for. There's no end to what we'll be able to do with that—' He broke off and sighed. 'Dreams . . . dreams . . .'

'They might let you film here,' Dorrie encouraged. 'If you asked them the right way.'

'Other hotels, possibly. But not the St Edmund's.' He shook his head. 'Too old and too snobbish. They don't need money—even if I had any to offer—and they don't need publicity. There's not a chance.'

'What a pity,' Dorrie commiserated, liking him more every minute.

'And what a waste!' He brooded over the marble staircase, the ornate moulded ceiling, the glittering crystal chandelier. 'You could really *do* something here — and there's plenty of room for a film crew, which is something else you don't often find.'

'It's selfish of them.' Dorrie was thoroughly on his side now. 'And, as you say, it's such a waste. I know I'd just love to watch a leading lady make an entrance down that staircase. It would be something to see.'

'It would indeed.' His gaze started at the upper landing and travelled slowly down the staircase as though following a stately progress.

'I couldn't help hearing you tell Lucy she had a lovely bone structure,' Dorrie said slyly. 'Funny that should be her name, isn't it? Lucy Bone with the lovely bones.'

'Oh?' He turned to her quickly. 'It's that obvious, is it?'

'No, no,' Dorrie denied quickly, but her mind was already racing ahead. Lucy Bone was such a plain name, almost ugly, for such a pretty girl. *Lucy Adair*. Mentally she tested the new name for suitability. It sounded *much* better.

'Look,' he said. 'I don't know how to explain this to you. It was just a passing thought, that's all.' His gaze returned to the staircase thoughtfully. 'Besides — ' he was elaborately offhand — 'she's pretty tied up with that Arab fellow, isn't she? They seem thick as thieves.'

'But thieves fall out,' Dorrie said.

'You're a disgraceful old matchmaker!' But he couldn't help laughing.

'I'm not,' she denied automatically. 'I just think she's too nice a girl to get tied up with a type like that.' She shuddered. 'He frightens me.'

'He frightened me, too, last night,' Tony admitted, abruptly serious. 'I couldn't let him see it, of course.'

'If you ask me,' Dorrie said, 'he's a very nasty customer.' She looked at him in surprise as he laughed again.

'I'm sorry,' he apologized. 'It was just — *customer* is so

apt! When we're all waiting outside Bonnard's for the sale to begin.'

'I didn't think of that.' She smiled reluctantly, hoping it wouldn't weaken her case. 'I just don't like him.'

'Neither do I.' He was serious again. 'However, he seems to be the lady's choice and I don't see what either of us can do about it. We might not approve of her taste but, essentially, it's none of our business.

Oh dear! Dorrie restrained a sigh. He didn't seem disposed to go out and fight for his lady fair. That was the trouble these days, everybody was too conscious of everybody else's point of view. If you asked her, there was a bit *too* much live-and-let-live in today's attitudes. That old competitive spirit was missing. There were people who thought that a good thing, but she wasn't so sure herself. It just seemed to flatten life out, somehow.

'On the other hand . . .' he said reflectively.

'Shh!' Over his shoulder, Dorrie could see Lucy Bone advancing towards them.

'Ideal for filming . . .' He picked up her cue and changed conversational gear effortlessly, turning slightly as he did so, and nodding to Lucy, so that it was unclear whether he was speaking about the St Edmund's or the girl.

Lucy hesitated uncertainly, nodded to them both, and continued on her way, her back betraying that she was conscious of the eyes focused on her.

'Doesn't she walk down the stairs beautifully?' Dorrie asked meaningfully. 'She couldn't do better if she had a book on her head.'

The rest of the queue were stirring when Dorrie returned. She slid her hot-water bottle into her sleeping-bag and followed it half way, propping herself up with cushions to read for a while and make an early breakfast out of the freshly-filled Thermos of tea and remaining rock cakes. Later, when the nearby cafés were open, she'd roam off and treat herself to a proper breakfast. It was the sort of day when bacon and eggs and fried tomato, with lots of toast and marmalade and a big strong pot of tea would just hit the spot.

Next to her, Zoltan yawned, opened his eyes, blinked, rolled over and, still encased in his blankets, proceeded to do a series of press-ups that threatened to overturn his camp bed. Dorrie stared in amazement; this was a new wrinkle.

'I must be fit.' Turning his head, Zoltan caught her eye and explained. 'The Sale starts tomorrow. I must be in top shape and ready.'

'I'm sure you needn't worry about that,' Dorrie said faintly. 'You look in the pink of condition to me.'

'You are not an expert.' He dismissed her opinion brusquely and went back to his exercises.

'I never claimed to be.' Dorrie turned away. Really, this was a miserable queue; it was not going to become one of her favourite memories. It wasn't nearly so nice as the Skytrain queue that time, with all the Americans.

Remembering, Dorrie realized that what was missing was the good humour. Apart from Tony Adair, no one in this queue made little jokes and all the friendliness was somehow missing. Perhaps if she'd been next to Faye and Tim, it would have been better, instead of having Zoltan in between. Or if Tony Adair had been immediately behind Lucy instead of that scowling killjoy, Sakim.

Faye and Tim were prepared to be friendly, but it was awkward. At the beginning, they had tried to get a game of Scrabble going, but Zoltan had had to be included and his command of English, while quite good, had not extended to the obscure words they produced and he had challenged everything to the point where the game had ceased to be fun, or even good-tempered. They had then turned to the Monopoly set but, here again, Zoltan had behaved with a single-minded determination to win that

had ruined everyone's enjoyment. You'd have thought he
was using real money and actually believed he was buying
up Park Lane and all those hotels. Perhaps he was using
the board as a training ground for the future ambitions
he undoubtedly harboured, but it made him an uncomfortable player when the others only wanted a bit of
amusement. In the end, Faye and Tim had given up and
retreated into a private world of quiet conversation and
reading. Dorrie had seen a pack of cards in their possession, but they had not brought them out and suggested a
game. Not that she could blame them. If Zoltan could get
so intense over Scrabble and Monopoly, the way he might
behave in a card game didn't bear thinking about.

Lucy Bone would probably be friendlier — if that Sakim
would let her. But every time she began a conversation,
he interrupted, jealous of any claim on her attention.

Tony Adair was really nice, but those silly newcomers
didn't seem to realize their luck. Just look at that
ridiculous makeshift barrier they had placed between
themselves and everyone else. She couldn't think they
were going to be a worthwhile addition to the queue.

It was a pity things couldn't have been different, but
today was the last day and there was no use grumbling —
not even silently to oneself. Dorrie sighed, pulled out her
book and escaped to the frozen Arctic wastes.

They day dragged on, seeming to move more slowly than the ones that had gone before it, for all that it was the last day they'd be sitting in the queue.

Perhaps that was why. Already the temper of the queue was changing. It wasn't just the sudden athletic preparations of Zoltan. Lucy Bone was abstracted and on edge; Sakim more morose than ever.

It will be all right, dear, Dorrie wanted to say to Lucy. But how could she, with Zoltan ready to pounce on every stray remark? She contented herself with a smile and a nod to the girl, who ignored both and disappeared back into her sleeping-bag, obviously fed up with everything and everyone.

Faye and Tim had gone off together to get an early lunch. Only Tony Adair seemed the same as ever, but he was deeply absorbed in making notes on a large sheaf of paper, lost to anything going on around him.

Not that much was going on. The newcomers were not now disposed to being friendly — not even to each other. They had the glazed unheeding look of people who were not accustomed to sitting up all night. They held magazines which they stared at unseeingly. When one made a comment, the other retorted so sharply it seemed they must be at daggers drawn rather than distracted with fatigue. It seemed quite probable that they would not stay the course through to another morning.

They'd be small loss. With a mental shrug, Dorrie tried to dismiss them from her thoughts, but could not quite succeed. After all, they might manage to hang on until the Sale started and no one had yet discovered what they were queuing for. Were they a threat to the aims of someone already in the queue? Perhaps later they'd be in a better mood and someone could tactfully introduce the subject . . .

Engrossed in her thoughts, she had not been aware of the running footsteps until they halted in front of her.

'Auntie Dorrie!' Young Ron was breathless and beaming. 'I've got what you want!' He flourished his satchel triumphantly.

'Don't shout, dear,' Dorrie said quickly. 'I can hear you perfectly well.' She darted a guilty sideways look at Zoltan to find him observing the scene with his usual lofty condescension.

'And I've brought you cakes and hot macaroni cheese . . .' He began unpacking his satchel, passing over the delights within as he enumerated them.

Dorrie swiftly took possession of the half-bottle of cherry brandy and the tiny phial he next held out to her.

'Mum says—' He was abruptly recalled to duty. 'Mum says, are you sure you're all right?' He waited with concern for her answer.

'Bless you, of course, I am. I'm right as rain.' She tucked the phial away at the bottom of her handbag.

'Mum says, if you're not, you're not to dream of staying in the queue. She says it's not worth you getting sick. Nothing's worth that and you're not to be silly. If you're not *perfectly* well, you're to pack it in and come home with me now.' He stepped back and inspected her anxiously, as though afraid she might suddenly fall to pieces at his feet. 'Are you *perfectly* well?'

'I'm *perfectly* well,' she assured him solemnly. 'You thank your mother and tell her not to worry.' It was too bad Sandra had frightened him, but it occurred to her that Sandra might be frightened herself. But there hadn't been time to explain—not that Dorrie had wanted to. She was rather hoping that she might never be called upon to account for this particular action.

If it happened. She was not committed in any way, she

reminded herself. Just because she had something, it didn't mean she had to use it.

'Well, then . . .' Young Ron seemed soothed, both by his inspection and her reassurances. 'If you're going to stay in the queue anyway, would you get something for me? Please? *After* you've got the fridge-freezer for Mum and Dad,' he added hastily.

'I'm sure I could manage. That is . . .' Belated caution set in. 'What is it you want?'

'Oh, there's plenty of them,' he said equally cautious, ready to start pussyfooting around the subject.

'Plenty of what?' She might not have had any children of her own, as it happened, but she knew their ways. And this one had begun exhibiting elaborate concern as he tried to sidestep the issue.

'You're going to have to tell me, you know,' she reminded him. 'Otherwise, I won't be able to buy it for you.'

'Oh, I've got the money.' He delved into his pockets eagerly, bringing out handfuls of silver. 'I've saved it out of my pocket money. One pound fifty.'

'Well . . .' Against her better judgement, she let him pour the money into her cupped hands. 'What is it you want?'

'Oh, uh . . .' He looked from Lucy to Zoltan, as though for help. They were watching him in fascination, but unable to provide anything except moral support. Lucy nodded to him encouragingly.

'It isn't much,' he said defensively. 'And they won't be hard to carry, at all. They'll fit right into your carrier bag and they don't weigh much.'

'That's fine,' Dorrie said sternly. 'Now what are they?'

'A . . . a pair of roller-skates.' It was out at last. He watched anxiously for her reaction.

'Ooo-er! And what does your mother think about that? Did she say you could have them?'

'No-o-o . . .' He wavered before her steady gaze, then

rallied. 'But she didn't say I couldn't,' he argued

Behind him, Zoltan grinned broadly — the first genuine enjoyment he had ever displayed. He met Dorrie's eyes and deliberately gave her a wicked wink.

Dorrie bit her lip, fighting against amusement. But really, you had to laugh. Besides, it could have been worse. She remembered roller-skates from her own childhood. They were a lot better — and safer — than those nasty skateboards. You never had to get rigged out in crash helmets and elbow pads and knee pads when you strapped on your skates. Your feet might shoot off in different directions but at least you were more likely to land where nature had intended — and had already provided ample padding.

'It will be all right,' Ron pleaded. 'Once I've got them. Please . . .' He stared at her trustingly.

'Well . . .' Dorrie capitulated slowly. 'I suppose they can't do you much harm . . .'

'Oh, thank you, Auntie Dorrie!' A quick, impulsive hug and he was darting off down the street before she could change her mind. She'd promised now — and could only hope that Sandra wouldn't be too upset about it.'

'That young man will go far, I think.' Zoltan nodded. 'He has the gift of getting his own way. In this world it is, perhaps, the most important gift one can have.'

'That's as may be.' Dorrie looked at him without liking. 'But it's just as well if you can get what you want without getting other people into trouble because of it.'

Foster gauged his time carefully. He had the small bundle of invitations, each addressed personally to its recipient. By the names they admitted to publicly.

Lucy Bone, indeed! He sniffed, but had adjudged it wiser not to force the issue. Could she keep up such a senseless pretence in front of Old Foster, who had ridden her through the store on his shoulders in her earliest days, who had ceremonially escorted her to Santa's Grotto in the days when she presided over the Childrens' Christmas Party, who knew her as well as he did his own grand-children — and was nearly as fond of her?

No, the international politicians had the right idea. If possible, it was better to avoid a face-to-face confron-tation. That way, everyone could save face.

So he waited for the afternoon torpor to set in. There was plenty of time. The cocktail-party was scheduled from six to eight or eight-thirty, or so. Plenty of time. They weren't going anywhere else.

For a long time, his vigil seemed hopeless. Although the others settled down into a half-dozing state, Lucy Bone remained wide awake and restless. Twitchy, almost. Compared with everyone else, that is.

Even that undesirable boy-friend of hers, crouching in that heathen attitude, had lowered his head to his chest, closed his eyes and opted out. Whether in sleep or medi-tation, it was impossible to say. Either way, it did not deflect Foster's animosity.

Getting plenty of rest before your shoplifting spree tomorrow? Oh, I know your type, my lad. I've dealt with enough of you over the past few years. And what our little Lucinda is doing, taking up with someone like you, beats me. She's too trusting by half, that's her trouble. Hasn't seen nearly enough of the world to understand what that sort can be like . . .

Needs to be shown what's what.

Someone like that. Waiting for the Sale to start, waiting to take advantage when he thinks Security can't be everywhere at once. Ready to rush in with the crowds, snatch everything he can get away with while the sales-people are waiting on the legitimate customers.

Oh, I've met your sort before, my lad. But you won't get away with it. Because, wherever you go, I'll be right there behind you. Dogging your footsteps, waiting to catch you in the act, waiting to show you up, charge you. We'll see how long that swagger of yours will last in Marlborough Street Magistrates' Court, when you're up before the beak with all the rest of your rotten lot.

And we'll see if our little Lucinda is so anxious to be associated with you after that. She's a Bonnard, after all, and the store still means something to her. It must, even though we haven't seen much of her around here lately . . .

Foster drifted off into a happy daydream in which he apprehended Sakim raiding the Jewellery Department, to Lucinda's amazement and horror.

'*Oh, Foster, I never knew he was like that.*' Tears trembled on her long soft lashes, her eyes were wide with injured innocence. '*He told me he was here to help carry my shopping.*'

'*Now, now, little Cinders.*' (Their private joke from away back.) '*That's the way the world is, outside there, with people who aren't your own sort. Bonnard's means nothing to him, nothing but a great covered-over Euro-pean bazaar to suck as though he'd landed with Genghis Khan and it was his by right of conquest. They think different to us, these people, you know—*'

'*Yes, yes, I understand that now, Foster. Thanks to you—*'

Beyond the plate-glass entrance door, back there in the queue, Lucy Bone lifted her head and directed a sudden unguarded look of such hostility at the entrance that Foster stepped back involuntarily, his pleasant dreams shattered.

She couldn't have seen him watching her, could she? No. No. He soothed his fears. Not possibly. He knew how the glass doors reflected the afternoon light and he was standing well back out of sight. That look of implacable hatred could not have been meant for him.

If not, then . . . Surely, it couldn't be Bonnard's she hated so, could it? Then what was she doing, sitting out there for days in the queue, waiting for the glorious, memorable, Once-in-a-Hundred-Years Sale to begin?

For the first time, the disquiet already rampaging through the Executive Floor swept over him. What did she want? What was she out there for?

It was unthinkable! His formerly pleasant daydream returned, transformed into a nightmare. Such things *had* happened. The private horrors encountered by staff and security guards in other stores rose before him.

The two of them, in an unholy alliance— *both* of them out on a shoplifting spree. Little Lucinda pillaging her father's store—silently daring the staff who had known her from childhood to do anything about it.

Suppose that was what he discovered when he dogged the dark boy's footsteps through the store? Suppose it was Lucinda's little white fingers closing around the pearl necklace, palming the diamond clip?

What was poor old Foster to do then?

His hand closing around her delicate wrist . . . the pain in his heart . . . the snarl on her face . . . the hate in her eyes.

And perhaps her boy-friend was carrying a knife. That sort often did . . .

It couldn't be true! Lucinda Bonnard behaving like that? Yet she was out there with a group of strangers, needlessly queuing, when she could have anything her heart desired just by asking her father for it. So why didn't she? What was she doing out there?

Could it be that all she really desired was to cause a scandal that would rock Bonnard's to its very foundations?

Sudden movement in the queue brought Foster out of his unhappy reverie.

Lucy Bone was wriggling out of her sleeping-bag, standing up, exchanging a few words with Sakim and then starting across the street.   •

As soon as Lucy Bone was safely inside the St Edmund's, Foster moved swiftly.

'Why, whatever's this?' Dorrie voiced the surprise of everyone as the crisp white envelopes were delivered into their hands.

'Open it and find out.' Foster winked amiably at her. He enjoyed knowing that he was bringing pleasant news. Too bad the Arab had to be included in the invitations — and he wasn't quite sure that the two newcomers at the end of the queue should have been invited. But Lucien Bonnard had ruled that the entire queue should be invited and there were crisp white envelopes for them, too.

He gave them their invitations and turned back just in time to see Sakim's hand snaking towards the invitation he had propped up on the flap of Lucy Bone's sleeping-bag to await her return.

Not going to let her see it — trying to keep it from her! The knowledge flashed through his mind instantly.

Sakim was quick but Foster, fired by indignation, was quicker. He stooped and snatched up the invitation just before Sakim's hand reached it.

Foster straightened triumphantly and looked around. Dorrie had been watching the scene and she met his eyes with a tiny approving nod. She, too, knew what was going on.

'Perhaps, madam — ' Foster handed her the invitation with a slight bow — 'you'd be good enough to see that this reaches the young lady?'

'You needn't worry.' Dorrie took the envelope with a meaning sidelong glance at Sakim. 'I'll most certainly see that she gets it personally.'

'Thank you, madam.' Foster smiled. They understood each other perfectly.

He was just closing the entrance door behind him when he heard a squeal of dismay. He turned to see Faye and

Dorrie looking at each other in consternation while the men stared at them uncomprehendingly.

They spoke in unison: 'I haven't a thing to wear!'

CHAPTER 14

'I'm not going,' Lucy Bone said.

'We all felt like that at first, dear,' Dorrie soothed. 'But then we thought it over and realized that of course they won't expect us to dress up. They know we can't run home and get changed. We'll just freshen up a bit at the St Edmund's and go the way we are.'

Lucy shook her head impatiently. They didn't understand at all and she couldn't explain — not without giving the game away. And there was no question of that. They were too close to success. 'I can't.' She shook her head again despairingly.

'Of course you can,' Tony Adair said sternly. 'See here, Bonnard's are making a big thing out of their Centenary Year. This Sale is the first event of the year, I think it's fantastic of them to do this. They're calling it an impromptu cocktail-party, but I'll bet you they've laid on all the trimmings. Just for us — and it would be churlish to refuse. *Any* of us!'

Behind him, the newcomers twittered agreement, thrilled to the marrow. How clever it had been of them to insist on joining the queue early. And wouldn't Geoff and Dave be green with jealousy at discovering what they'd missed? A private party in Bonnard's Executive Suite! It was worth every bit of the lost sleep and discomfort. They'd dine out on this for years *and* it would be a story for the grandchildren when they eventually appeared. But how unfortunate if there was going to be a dissenter to spoil the fun.

'It will just be a sort of "Come-As-You-Are" party.' Dorrie was still trying to reassure Lucy. 'That's what the nice American lady told us.'

Nice American lady? Dirty usurping bitch! The force of her fury shook Lucy. She dipped her head so that the expression on her face might not betray her.

'The commissionaire who gave out the invitations sent her down to talk to us when he thought we might be a bit upset,' Dorrie went on. 'About not having the right thing to wear,' she explained. 'Such a pity you were over in the St Edmund's when it happened. You missed it all.'

Foster—dear Foster. The thought caught Lucy unawares and she repudiated it instantly. *Nosey, interfering Foster! Up to his usual boot-licking tricks.* Why, then, should she have this sudden catch in her throat, this feeling of wanting to weep for the times that had been, the past that could never return again?

'She does not wish to attend the party,' Sakim said harshly. 'Neither do I. There is no law that says we must.'

He should have kept his stupid mouth shut! He never knew when to keep quiet. Everyone else in the queue looked at him with dislike, then—too obviously—tried to make allowances. Even the other foreigner, who might have been expected to understand, if not sympathize.

'It is all right,' Zoltan said. 'Arrangements have been made. One of the security guards—with his dog—will come out and patrol the queue while we are inside. We can safely leave our things, they will not be touched. Nor will anyone be allowed to take our places in our absence. There is nothing to be concerned about. Bonnard's have thought of everything.'

They didn't understand a thing! Lucy bit down on rising hysteria. *Not one single thing!*

'I must say,' the newcomer called Janice remarked, 'I don't think it's very polite to refuse the invitation when Bonnard's have gone to all that trouble for us.'

For them? The woman wouldn't be quite so smug if she knew the real reason Bonnard's was rolling out the red carpet. Or trying to.

'I won't go,' Lucy said again.

'If you're not feeling well, dear,' Dorrie said, 'why don't you take a little nap? It's still a couple of hours before the party starts. You'll feel a lot better by then.'

'Oh!' Lucy wriggled down into her sleeping-bag and pulled the flap over her head.

Irritatingly, Tony Adair had not said one further word to try to make her change her mind.

Maggie hesitated outside the door, aware that Lucien was pacing the floor. He hadn't done that for a long time. In the early days, when she first came to work at Bonnard's, it had been a nervous habit of his. As their relationship had begun and progressed, however, most of his nervous habits had disappeared.

Until his darling daughter had started acting up again.

Maggie had a sudden picture of herself, standing outside the door like a suppliant. Rather, like a staff member afraid of a reprimand for some misdemeanour.

In sharp annoyance at herself she moved swiftly, tapping at the door and opening it in the same motion. Lucien turned from the window as she entered.

'Pre-party nerves?' she asked brightly.

'A bit.' He didn't pretend to misunderstand, which was an improvement. There were too many moments lately when Lucien seemed a stranger, distant and coldly polite, lost in thoughts she could not share.

'No need. Everything's arranged. The bar is all set up in the Boardroom and the kitchen is doing a hot buffet — enough for three times the number, from what I could see.'

'My instructions,' Lucien said. 'People can always eat more in cold weather. They need more, and I don't —' He broke off, but Maggie could finish the sentence in her own mind.

And I don't know when Lucinda will get a decent meal again.

Tomorrow he would lose sight of her again. Once the Sale had opened and she had done whatever she had come here for, she would vanish once more into that uncharted mysterious underground that seemed to exist in order to absorb the rebels of society into its ranks without trace.

'I don't even know if she'll come.' Lucien swerved aside from his own thought.

I. When they were planning the party, he'd said '*we*'. She was losing him already. He was slipping away from her, back into a world he had inhabited before she came along. The fact that it had been an unhappy world did not prevent him from returning to it. Familiarity had its attractions, too.

'*Everyone* is coming,' Maggie assured him, with more conviction than she felt.

The little bitch is trying to drive him into a coronary. But she could not be allowed to succeed.

'If she does come—' Lucien faced Maggie with unaccustomed helplessness—'what do I say to her?'

A good question. What should he do? Apologize for being alive and a human being? For wanting a life of his own? For daring to think of a new wife, a new family?

'You could suggest she see a psychiatrist.' It popped out before she had a chance to stop it, before she had a chance to think.

Lucien turned away. As might be expected, he was not amused.

Not that it was really funny. Maggie felt an overpowering resentment. The girl was poisoning all their lives. It was bad enough that Lucien had lost all sense of proportion over the girl; it was too much that her own sense of humour should also be affected. The months since Lucinda had disappeared had been difficult; now that she had reappeared, things had become more difficult still.

Lucien stood immovable at the window, looking down

as though sufficient concentration might enable him to see through the overhanging permanent canopy and watch the people in the queue. Watch Lucinda.

Persona non grata again. She was getting used to it, but she didn't like the feeling. Maggie battled with her emotions; this was no time to let her ego surface. If she started a fight with Lucien now, with the mood they were both in, there was no telling where it might lead.

'I thought we might have the February Exhibition on display in the Boardroom as well,' Lucien said. 'It would be an additional little talking point for them to have a preview of it. Everyone enjoys looking at jewellery and medals. Would you see to it?'

'I'll see to it,' Maggie said. It would also be a last desperate throw of the dice to try to remind Lucinda of her proud heritage. But it was odds-on that the queue would be more impressed than she was.

'Good idea,' Maggie added, but he did not respond.

Maggie wrenched her gaze away from Lucien's obdurate back. She looked at the desk for distraction, but the desk was clear in preparation for a party which might spill over into other offices. People looking for rest rooms often wandered innocently through closed doors into private offices.

Almost clear. The leather folder of photographs still stood at one corner of the desk. Two women laughed out of it. The dead woman there was no point in being jealous of—and a younger, idealized version of the darling daughter, all adoration and innocence. Before the rot set in. But this was the way Lucien remembered her, the way he wanted to remember her. It might be a very salutary experience for him to have a long close look at the brat now—and also the shifty boy-friend who had replaced him in her affections.

Perhaps then Lucien might begin looking to the future. Perhaps he might even put Maggie's picture on his desk.

Or was there some quaint old English tradition that said such a move had to wait until after the official ceremony?

If she couldn't keep her big mouth shut, there might not be a ceremony.; Maggie grimaced wryly to herself. *'Feelings are running high in this here town, pardner . . .'* It was time for strangers—and even friends and lovers—to keep a low profile.

Maggie picked up the leather folder and flipped it shut. As Lucien turned from the window, she held it out to him.

'You'd better put this away.' She kept her voice carefully neutral. 'I don't think "Lucy Bone" would be pleased if the others were to discover her real identity.'

'It doesn't matter.' He took the folder from her and tossed it into a drawer with a sigh of defeat. 'She won't come.'

CHAPTER 16

So this was what was behind the scenes at Bonnard's. Dorrie looked around avidly.

An enormous table had been pushed against one wall and covered with a white linen cloth. Against the opposite wall stood a row of display cases with intriguing glittering contents connected by coloured ribbons to strange-looking maps mounted on the wall above them.

The walls themselves were covered with swirled walnut panelling with indirect lighting provided by frosted-glass sconces at intervals along them. It looked as though successive layers of Edwardian and Art Deco modernity had been overlaid on the original Victorian design without either disguising or defeating it. The age of the faded but still-glowing Persian carpet on the floor was something only to be guessed at. Like Bonnard's itself, the room bespoke luxury, enduring elegance and good solid value.

'Very nice.' Beside her, Zoltan was radiating approval of all he surveyed. 'Very civilized.' You didn't have to be a mind-reader to know that he was picturing himself at the head of a big table like that some day, presiding over a Board of Directors meeting. It wouldn't surprise her if he made it, either. He was sharp enough — and just about shifty enough.

Not that she thought there was anything shifty about Bonnard's. Not these days, anyway. But perhaps once — when they'd started out — someone had had to have a bit extra in the way of ambition, and the cleverness to go with it, to bring the whole thing into being.

Absently she followed Faye and Tim as they walked along, quite as though they'd been here before and were familiar with the routine. She saw them exchange words with a pleasant-looking woman and move on to shake hands with the distinguished man standing beside her.

Then, suddenly, it was her turn — and she was shaking hands with Lucien Bonnard himself. 'Oh, Mr Bonnard,' she gasped, quite overcome. 'I'm so pleased to meet you. I just *love* your store.'

Behind her, she heard Zoltan snort with amusement and immediately wished the floor would open up and swallow her. She had said the wrong thing again. But what *did* you say to the owner of a store?

'Thank you.' Lucien Bonnard smiled, murmuring his acknowledgement. If she had been rude, it didn't seem to have bothered him. Indeed, he seemed not to have noticed it. Dorrie moved along gratefully to catch up with Faye and Tim, but she couldn't help glancing back.

'A nice place you have here,' was evidently Zoltan's idea of *savoir-faire*. 'Very nice indeed.' He gave an approving nod, man-to-man, as he shook hands with Lucien Bonnard.

Dorrie immediately felt better. She had caught the faint ripple of disdain across Lucien Bonnard's face. At least he hadn't looked like that when she'd made *her* comment.

'I'm glad you like it,' Lucien Bonnard said drily.

Surely Zoltan couldn't be so thick-skinned that he missed the nuances in his host's tone? However, he moved to join the others with an assured swagger that suggested that he was the only one among them who had risen suitably to the occasion.

Covered silver serving dishes reflected the glow of the tall lighted candles along the tables. Fresh flowers clustered in lustrous silver vases. Waitresses hurried to serve their drinks. No expense of effort had been spared — and all for them.

Dorrie gave a mental sigh for the designer gown she'd bought in that Kensington sale two years ago. It would have been perfect to wear on this occasion. But there you were, you couldn't pack for a queue as though you were going on a cruise. You couldn't know that this would happen. There had never been anything like it before and probably never would be again. Stores didn't have hundredth anniversaries all that often.

'What a shame the others wouldn't come,' Faye said. 'They don't know what they're missing.'

'I wouldn't give up on Lucy Bone just yet,' Dorrie said. 'I had a word with that young lady just before we came inside.' She gave an emphatic nod. 'I put a flea in her ear and I wouldn't be surprised but what she'll come round once she's had a chance to think it over.'

'I hope so,' Faye said. 'It will be *too* bad if she lets that ghastly boy-friend of hers browbeat her into losing out on all the fun. Although,' she added thoughtfully, 'I'd be surprised if it were the first time he'd done it.'

'So would I.' Dorrie glanced automatically towards the door, but there was no sign of Lucy Bone yet. She noticed that Lucien Bonnard was greeting the last of his guests, while looking over their shoulders in a faintly puzzled manner. So he, too, was aware of the discourtesy of the queue. They would have to try to make it up to him by extra appreciation of all the trouble he had gone to for them.

'Let's look over here—' The sign surmounting the display cases explained that this was a Private View of the main Centenary Exhibition to be unveiled next month. They gazed raptly at the exhibits so encrusted with gems that they seemed more jewellery than medals and Orders. 'They must be worth a king's ransom,' Dorrie murmured in awe.

'Isn't it exciting?' The suburban ladies joined them, completely at ease and ready to be friendly now, evidently considering that they were all guests in Bonnard's Boardroom and this constituted a proper introduction and possibly even a guarantee of *bona fides*. 'I'm so pleased we got into the queue early. Wait until I tell Geoff about this—he'll be livid that he didn't come along! I was saying to Gwen, this is so super I won't even mind if we don't get anything at all in the Sale. It's all been worth it just for this!'

'What *are* you queuing for?' Dorrie nipped in sharply, taking advantage of the euphoria. 'Some of us were wondering.'

'Oh, nothing special,' Janice said. 'Possibly one of those designer suits and some of the china. They have such good things, haven't they?'

Opportunists. Dorrie barely restrained a sniff. There were plenty of them at every sale, although they didn't usually bother to queue beforehand.

'And then we thought we'd just wander through the store.' Unwittingly Gwen put the seal on Dorrie's identification. 'And see if there were any other good bargains we'd like to buy.'

'Very wise of you.' Dorrie allowed cordiality to creep in. 'You'll have the pick of everything in the sale.'

'That's why we decided to queue,' Janice agreed. 'The earliest train wouldn't get us here until after ten o'clock. We know because that's the way we usually do it. But this time, we decided to be different and join the queue. We've never,' she added unnecessarily, 'done anything like this before.'

'Nor have I,' Zoltan put in. He looked around with satisfaction. 'But now I shall do it again.'

'Of course, something like this doesn't happen every time,' Dorrie cautioned. 'In fact, I've never seen it before—and you might call me an expert on queues.'

'If you're not, I don't know anyone else who could be called one.' Tony Adair came up to them, he had been wandering around the room taking in all the details. He shook his head. 'God—what a set! I'd love to use it for a

128

film. Except, of course—' he grinned ruefully—'I haven't a script that would be remotely suitable.'

'You and your films,' Dorrie said indulgently. 'They're all you think about.'

'Not quite all.' As though it had reminded him, he turned to look at the door.

The host and hostess were conferring anxiously together, glancing towards their guests and then turning back to each other. Lucien Bonnard, in particular, seemed dissatisfied. The woman appeared to be trying to cheer him up.

'It was a gamble, Lucien,' she said. 'We both knew it. It was always on the cards that she might refuse.'

'I know.' He had to restrain himself from crossing to the door and looking down the empty corridor. 'But, since she'd come this far, it seemed possible . . .' He shrugged.

'We have guests,' Maggie reminded him. 'We ought to mingle.' She took his arm and led him away from the doorway.

Faye and Tim were admiring the only painting in the room that wasn't one of the Bonnard ancestors looking down on the deliberations of the Board. A small but perfect beach scene somewhere on the French coast in the late 1800's.

'It's by Pierre Bonnard, isn't it?' Tim asked as Lucien and Maggie approached. 'Was he a relation?'

'We'd like to think so—' Lucien shrugged deprecatingly—'but no one is entirely sure. Not a terribly close connection, in any case. A distant cousin, perhaps.'

'Given the size of the population in those days,' Faye said. 'It's almost certain there'd be a link. The same names recur again and again and you can almost count on their being the same family, if you trace it back far enough.'

'That's a thought,' Maggie put in. 'Have you ever had the family traced back, Lucien? We ought to do it some day.' The idea of discovering an artist on the ancestral tree was enticing. Another star in the rich inheritance they would hand on to their children, a cultural heritage as well as a mercantile one.

'We tend to leave that sort of thing to the Americans,' Lucien said. 'We don't go in for it much in England.'

'I *am* an American,' Maggie reminded him. 'And I think it's high time the Bonnards went in for it. Anyway, someone must have made a gesture towards it in the past, otherwise what are you doing with that painting in the first place?'

'My father bought it at an auction,' Lucien admitted. 'Perhaps he had intended to do something about tracing a link, but—' he shrugged—'the store kept him too busy. It keeps us all busy.'

She would get someone on to it before long, Maggie determined. She might even try it herself. It would be a pleasant way to while away the late stages of pregnancy when she presumably wouldn't feel like coming in to the store every day.

Unaware of his fiancé's benevolent scheming, Lucien exchanged a few more smiling remarks with the Moores before moving on. They were a pleasant young couple, but they had led the queue and were hence valueless for his purposes. He wanted to talk to someone who had been closer to Lucinda.

His target was talking to an amiable-looking young man, who had also occupied the wrong place in the queue so far as he was concerned.

'Everything all right?' The question was automatic, as was the glance he swept over them to check that their glasses were topped up. They all looked happy and pleased with themselves—and with Bonnard's.

'Just lovely,' Dorrie said happily. 'It's so nice of you—'

'Not at all,' he cut her off.

'Our pleasure,' Maggie said warmly. 'We think it's pretty nice of you to give up your warm beds and queue up for days in this weather.'

'Oh, but we enjoy it,' Dorrie said quickly. 'At least,' she clarified, '*I* do.'

'It is her hobby.' Zoltan moved closer to Dorrie, ready to imply intimacy with anyone receiving attention from the head of Bonnard's. 'This is not the only queue she has joined.'

'Bless you, no,' Dorrie laughed. 'I've been in every queue in town at one time or another.' Then, realizing that her response might leave something to be desired, she added hastily, 'But this has been the . . . the most hospitable.'

She had just stopped short of saying 'nicest', but she couldn't have brought herself to utter such an untruth. *Some* of the people were all right, but the others were in danger of ruining it all.

'Bonnard's has the best of everything — even queues.' That Zoltan — always trying to curry favour — much good it might do him. Lucien Bonnard's eyelids flickered and he looked as though he might have been amused if he hadn't had something more important on his mind.

He seemed to be trying to think of something to say and Dorrie tried frantically to think of some bright remark to help him out, but her gaze drifted over his shoulder and she forgot him momentarily.

'There you are —' She turned triumphantly to the others. 'I *told* you she'd come!'

Lucien Bonnard spun to face the door, almost as though he knew what she was talking about.

She shouldn't have come. Lucy hesitated in the doorway, loath to advance into the expectant hush, yet equally unable to retreat because a glowering Sakim blocked her path.

It was all his fault. She hadn't been going to come, she had determined against it. He needn't have used any of his arguments, but then he had flourished the most fatal one of all: he had *forbidden* her to come.

That had done it! Without a backward glance, she had shrugged out of her sleeping-bag and marched straight to the staff entrance and the private lift to the executive floor, not even pausing long enough to fix her hair — not giving herself time to think.

She had been aware that Sakim was following one short step behind her — and good enough for him! That was the right place for him. He needn't think *she* was going to walk three paces behind *him*. Forbid, indeed!

Besides, as she would point out when she made her peace with him later, it was as well to check their line of retreat. Things might have changed since the last time she had been in here. People moved offices, doors might have been blocked off, whole areas could have been renovated and redesigned, rendering her memories useless. Although, really, it seemed that nothing had changed.

Maggie and Lucien started forward as one, then halted abruptly, obviously unsure of the line they should take now that she had actually appeared.

'There's the rest of our queue!' Dorrie came forward to take her by the hand. 'Come and meet Mr Bonnard, dear,' she said loudly. 'He's our host, you know.' More quietly, she added, 'I'm so pleased you changed your mind. You're right, you know, to come. It wouldn't have been proper if you hadn't.' She gave Sakim a cool nod, in no doubt as to where the problem lay.

Peer pressure. That was part of it, Lucy recognized. Although once she would never have thought of this motley collection as her peers. Not until she had spent several months with Sakim's peers.

Smiling gratefully, Lucy allowed Dorrie to capture her

hand and lead her forward. That was the right line to take: they were all strangers, united momentarily by the whim of a kindly host—one they had never met before and would never see again.

'How do you do?' She stared blankly and blandly into Lucien's eyes as Dorrie presented them, then moved aside so that Sakim could be introduced. Dorrie continued to do the honours, although noticeably more reluctantly.

Lucy relinquished Lucy's flaccid hand and managed barely to touch Sakim's fingertips, while drawing Maggie forward to be introduced in her turn.

The women eyed each other coldly—Maggie could look as blank as anyone when she put her mind to it. She hadn't lived in England all this time without learning how to put a touch of frost into her smile, either.

Before they could speak, Tony Adair swept down on Lucy. 'Good girl, you came! You won't regret it.' He winked companionably at Lucien Bonnard. 'Have you seen the spread they've laid on for us? Just come and look!' Gently he plucked her away from Sakim.

'Perhaps you'd be kind enough to help Miss Bone to a drink, Mr Adair,' Lucien said cordially. He hadn't missed the muffled growl of hatred from Sakim. Any wedge that might be driven between Lucinda and this—this *barbarian*—was to be encouraged.

'I'll bet I know what you've got your eye on—' Deftly, Dorrie blocked Sakim's path as he started after the pair. 'It's beautiful, isn't it? Don't you wish they had it in the Sale instead of the one you're after?'

He gave her the look that made her wonder if he understood English at all, even though she'd heard him speaking it. He tried to sidestep her, but she moved with him, still blocking him, giving Lucy and Tony time to reach the table and begin a conversation.

'The *carpet*,' she insisted. 'Isn't it the most perfect you've ever seen? I'll bet—' she caught Lucien's approving eye—'I'll bet it's—it's a genuine antique,' she finished hastily, blushing.

She'd nearly said, *I'll bet it cost a bomb*—and right in front of Lucien Bonnard, too.

'Very nice.' Sakim glanced perfunctorily towards his feet before lifting his glowering eyes to focus with burning intensity on the couple who had escaped him. He moved again, but this time Lucien Bonnard was swifter.

'You're interested in carpets?' he asked smoothly. 'The lady is correct, this one is an antique. Alas, I can never remember whether it's a Bokhara or not, nor eighteenth century or seventeenth. Perhaps you might identify it for me? It was an inheritance from my grandfather and his records were not always—'

'Excuse me,' Sakim said firmly. 'I must speak to my friend.' He turned on his heel, marched in a wide circle around them and moved towards Lucy.

'You know—' Dorrie stared after him thoughtfully—'I don't believe he knows anything about carpets at all.'

'Would that be so surprising?' Lucien asked.

'Well . . . perhaps not.' Dorrie gave a nervous little laugh. 'It's just that he's queuing for the Persian carpet in the window. For his mother . . . he says.' She discovered she now doubted that, as well. If he behaved the way he did to a sweet girl like Lucy Bone, was it likely that he was any nicer to his mother? She was beginning to suspect that Sakim had just enough wit to tell people what he thought they wanted to hear—but wasn't quite clever enough to keep them believing it. Probably, like Zoltan, he was buying to resell at a profit. At least Zoltan was honest about his intention. If Sakim had gauged the temper of the queue towards Zoltan, he had decided to lie about his own plans in order to get into their good graces.

Or was he lying to try to impress Lucy?

'I see how you could have made the mistake,' Maggie said. 'Of course it's a fallacy to think that someone is an expert on carpets just because he comes from that part of the world. You might as well expect all of us to be experts on heraldry or medieval monasteries just because there's so much of them around in England.'

'I know.' Dorrie was uncomfortably aware that her face was still red and this conversation wasn't helping any. 'I'm sorry. I suppose the truth of the matter is that I just don't like that man and I suppose I'm looking for excuses to justify myself.'

'He didn't appear,' Lucien said carefully, 'to be a particularly likeable person. Of course, I've just met him, whereas you've had the opportunity to study him for several days.'

'That's a fact!' Dorrie rose to the bait. 'And I like him even less than you do. It's not that I'm prejudiced—' She appealed to Lucien Bonnard— 'but I hate to see him with that nice young girl. She's far too good for him—and I'm sure he doesn't treat her properly.'

'Indeed?' Lucien Bonnard looked unexpectedly grim. It emboldened her or perhaps the cocktail she had chosen was stronger than she had thought—to confide in him further.

'Now that nice young English boy is more her style, I'd say. And I'm not just saying it because he's English. But he's intelligent and ambitious, and friendly with it. He's going places, that lad, and good luck to him—he deserves it. He's altogether more her sort and—' she lowered her voice—'he fancies her, I know. He says he'd like to film her, but there's more to it than that, I'll be bound!'

'Indeed?' Lucien Bonnard looked across the room with new interest and was just in time to see Lucinda throw back her head and laugh unexpectedly at something the young man had said to her. But at that moment Sakim's hand fell on her arm and the laughter was abruptly silenced. The glimpse of the delightful girl he had known vanished and the sulky stranger was in her place once more. Tony Adair looked after her, crestfallen, as Sakim drew her away.

'I just don't like him!' Unconsciously Dorrie echoed Lucien Bonnard's thought. 'I don't mind telling you, I've been doing everything I could to push her and Tony together and make her see how nasty Sakim really is. She's right behind me in the queue, you know, and I often have a chance to have a quiet word with her. And then, there's the times at the St Edmund's. Oh, I get my chance to slip a word in now and again—'

She broke off in sudden confusion as she realized just how thoroughly she was monopolizing the conversation. Although Mr Bonnard was so polite that he was bending forward as though he were hanging on her every word. What must he be thinking of her?

'Oh dear!' she said, blushing more furiously than ever. 'Just listen to me running on like this! You must think I'm a silly match-making old fool.'

'On the contrary,' Lucien Bonnard said warmly. 'I think you're absolutely wonderful.'

Curiously enough, he seemed to mean it.

CHAPTER 17

'Well,' Maggie said philosophically, surveying the wreckage of the buffet, 'You win some, you lose some. I think we could call it a draw on this one. You didn't get to talk to Lucinda alone, but you sure struck a gold-mine of information in the old duck next to her.'

'Very true,' Lucien agreed. 'In fact, my only regret is that I was unable to speak as long—and as freely—as I would have liked with Mrs Witson. She seemed a very perspicacious woman.'

'You mean, she was on our side,' Maggie corrected. 'Even though she didn't know it. Long may she rave! And may Lucinda listen to her. Sometimes a stranger can get through when those nearest and dearest aren't able to.'

'I may be Lucinda's nearest,' Lucien said drily, 'but I doubt that I'm her dearest.'

'Lucien—' Maggie wrapped her arms around him, willing him not to pull away. He was always half a stranger to her after an encounter with his daughter. Perhaps that was the reason she could not wholeheartedly wish him well in his ambition to draw Lucinda back into the bosom of the family. That family was irrevocably dissolved now; her own family not yet started. Perhaps there must always be an element of rivalry between the two. Perhaps this was something Lucinda had recognised earlier—and far more clearly—than she had.

'So near and yet so far,' Lucien brooded. 'Which was precisely what my darling daughter intended to convey to me. We still have no indication why she's really waiting out there in the queue.'

'We tried.' Maggie's arms fell away. *And we failed.* What kind of consolation would that be to Lucien when whatever scandal Lucinda was plotting broke over him.

She shuddered abruptly. *Someone walked over my grave. And I know who'd like to dance on it!*

She could not dismiss the look of implacable enmity the girl had given her just before turning away. She was marked down as the Wicked Stepmother in a totally unfair assessment. Lucinda had never given her a chance, never really spoken to her. It was so damnably unfair. She was willing to bend over backwards to be friends with the girl, why wouldn't Lucinda unbend just a little herself?

'Yes,' Lucien said wearily. 'We tried.'

Maggie glanced at him quickly, realizing that he had been berating himself silently, just as she had been.

Congratulations, Lucinda! You've succeeded in making everyone miserable again. And that's the reason you're out there, isn't it? . . . One of the reasons . . .

'Look, Lucien.' Maggie repressed the memory of those hate-filled eyes. 'She isn't totally hostile. Not to you. She proved that by coming to the party—'

'She didn't stay long.'

'Well, what did you expect her to do—lead the Hokey-Cokey?' Maggie bit down on her anger, apologizing immediately. 'I'm sorry, Lucien. I didn't mean—'

'You're upset,' he said. 'So am I. She always has this effect on us. Sometimes I think she wants to set us quarrelling between ourselves.'

At least he understood that much. He wasn't completely blinded by his daughter's stratagems. In his own way he was apologizing, too.

'Anyway, the others enjoyed the party.' She met him half way.

'The food was excellent, wasn't it?'

'How would you know? You barely touched it.' She looked at his drawn face with concern. 'Let me get you something now. Even with all they ate, there's still plenty left. The chef outdid himself with the Bœuf Stroganoff.'

'I'm not hungry.' Lucien shook his head. 'Thank you.'

'Look, Lucien,' she said helpfully. 'It might not be so bad. Figure it this way: we've got a full staff of Security people and extra ones hired for the duration of the Sale. We can have a couple of our own Security people standing by to spot her and tag after her as soon as she comes through the door. They can stay with her and, if she starts anything, they can just close in on her and spirit her behind the scenes quietly before she has a chance to make any sort of scene. I know you don't like the idea of having your own daughter spied on in your own store. But you've got to be practical.'

'Maggie —' he sank into his chair and leaned back, closing his eyes, refusing to look at her — 'Maggie, I believe I would like something to eat. Organize it for me, would you, please?'

Maggie — leave me!

'Of course.' She put on a bright smile, even though he wasn't looking and held it until the door closed behind her. The corridor was deserted as she crossed it quickly and went into the Boardroom where the remains of the party had not yet been cleared away.

She shut the door behind her and leaned against it, looking around the room to make sure it was empty. It was. She let the bright frozen smile dissolve and fumbled for her handkerchief.

'Wasn't it lovely?' Dorrie sighed ecstatically. 'Wasn't it a perfect dream? I always said, there never was a store like Bonnard's! Just imagine them doing all that for us!'

'Us and their hundredth anniversary,' Zoltan said. 'It is good public relations for them, They hope we will go away and tell everyone about it and it will spread goodwill for the store.'

'I certainly will tell everyone,' Dorrie said. 'They deserve all the goodwill they get.'

Lucy Bone made a curious noise deep in her throat, not quite a sob, nor a snort, nor a laugh. Dorrie decided to ignore it. The girl had come, after all, even though she hadn't lingered, and she'd brought her ghastly boy-friend along with her so that there'd be one hundred per cent attendance from the queue and honour was satisfied. Lucy Bone had made the effort, she was entitled to her own opinion.

It was too bad that her unpleasant boy-friend was still sulking, but it had to be admitted that his silences were preferable to his attempts at conversation. Nose out of joint, probably, because Lucy had spent so much time talking with Tony Adair—and had seemed to enjoy it.

'I'll not only tell all my friends about it,' Janice called over to Dorrie. 'From now on, I'll keep special watch to see what other stores have centenaries coming up.'

'I wouldn't bother if I were you,' Lucy Bone said. 'This isn't likely to happen again.'

'That's right,' Dorrie said. 'Not every store is Bonnard's. They do things proper here.'

'That's a fantastic collection of medals and honours they have,' Tony Adair said enthusiastically. 'Mr Bonnard has promised to let me film them next week before they go on public display in February. He says that if it turns out well, they may use some of the stills for publicity.'

'That's wonderful,' Dorrie said. 'I noticed you having a nice long talk with him after—' She broke off abruptly. She couldn't say 'after Lucy left', that would betray how closely she had been watching.

'Perhaps he'll let you do some more filming in the store,' she substituted hastily. 'You were telling me you'd love to film the Boardroom.'

'I told him that, too,' Tony said. 'And he said we'd talk about it. I tried to plant the idea that a short documentary about Bonnard's would be a good project for Centenary Year. Lots of businesses sponsor documen-

140

taries about their firms or products. I know I could do a good one and—'he grinned—'it would make a change from pestering the National Film Finance Corporation for grants. It would be bliss to have a commercial sponsor.'

'I wouldn't build too many hopes on it,' Lucy Bone warned.

'He meant it,' Tony said. 'He was definitely interested. I can tell.' He grinned wryly. 'I've talked to too many who weren't.'

'He might have been interested,' Lucy said. 'But a lot of things can happen—"

'You may be right.' Tony Adair laughed. 'But getting them interested is the hardest part. You're half way there, once they are.'

'I am thirsty.' Sakim rose from his heels abruptly and loomed between them, frowning down at Lucy.

Spoilsport! Dorrie looked at him with disfavour. Not that he'd care, even if he noticed. But the hint of romance reminded her.

'Perhaps they'll let you film the wedding,' she said.

'Wedding?' Tony's eyes brightened with interest. 'Whose?'

'Mr Bonnard and that nice American lady. Didn't you hear the waitress telling us? They're getting married right after the Sale. Everybody's very happy for them, they make such a lovely couple. Him so distinguished-looking and her so— *Oh!*' She broke off in pain, drawing up her foot.

'I'm sorry,' Lucy apologized perfunctorily. She had risen in such haste that she had stumbled and trodden on the woman. At least, it had stopped her senseless monologue.

'I'm thirsty, too.' Lucy turned to Sakim. 'Let's get out of here and find something to drink.'

Where had it all gone wrong?

Lucien Bonnard had asked himself the question a thousand times.

Bonnard's—both as a store and as a family—had been riding high for so long that it had seemed as though they could weather any storm. Inextricably bound together, it had seemed as though they could never sink.

Partly through good management, partly through luck—never discount luck—they had continued successfully on their set course while other of the great Victorian emporia had foundered and gone under.

Bonnard's had pioneered the way in staff welfare. They had been among the first to set up and maintain staff hostels, subsidized canteens, winter holidays, profit-sharing schemes and flexitime. Other innovations which had not been so successful had been, with the agreement of the staff, quietly dropped.

Staff loyalty had blossomed, Bonnard's had flourished, its staff relations the envy of many other major stores. They had never had a strike; when there had been transport strikes, those coming from the outer suburbs had cheerfully doubled-up in rooms in the hostel or bedded down in the Furniture Department of Bonnard's itself. Over the decades, a sense of unity and camaraderie had taken root and grown. Bonnard's was an establishment, a tradition, a team to which they all belonged. They loved working there and enjoyed it, knowing that a Bonnard's employee was head-and-shoulders above any other employee of any other London store. They walked in pride and were certain that they had chosen the better way.

Perhaps they had all grown too complacent.

The Bonnard family had always been close and loving; the warmth had spilled over to include the store and the staff. Throughout the long years of its existence, Bonnard's staff had felt themselves to be part of the family and that feeling had been expressed in the continuity of service and courtesy extended to the decades of loyal customers. Customers who had been brought to

Bonnard's as children by their parents and grown up in the certain assurance that there was no store so good, so exclusive, so reliable as Bonnard's and who, in turn, had passed on this belief to their children and grandchildren. Of such things was tradition born. And tradition itself was a self-perpetuating force stretching out endlessly beyond the barriers of time and space. It had seemed that Bonnard's was set fair to go on for ever — certainly well beyond Lucien Bonnard's own lifetime and that of his children . . . child.

Where had it all gone wrong?

Through successive recessions, depressions and two World Wars, the Bonnard pennant had flown high and proudly over the store.

But . . . *'Trees die at the top'* . . . *'Dying fish go rotten from the head downwards'* . . .

He didn't want to believe the old sayings. He didn't even want to think about them. But he could not avoid it. Were they true?

Was it something he had done? Some intrinsic fault in himself?

The Bonnards had always sat so complacently on the sidelines, watching their competitors falter, if not fall. The Bonnards had spent many years congratulating themselves that they had escaped the pitfalls which had ensnared their rivals, if not their peers. With barely concealed glee, the Bonnards had watched as others had plunged into a maelstrom from which a Divine Providence — if not their own good common sense — had protected them. Not for them the excesses and follies of other entrepreneurial families.

They had in their beginning, in the infinite wisdom of Great-Great-Grandfather Bonnard, purchased the freehold of the property on which Bonnard's had been built. Not for them the siren snare of the 99-year lease on which so many Victorian fortunes had been founded, trusting in the implicit promise of a world that would go on as it had started, with reasonable rates, benevolent landlords and peppercorn rents prevailing for ever.

That was the major problem these days. From poor bewildered shops in the High Street to such institutions as Jackson's of Piccadilly, the 99-year leases were terminating in this past decade or so and the new rents were so prohibitive that a store could not pay them and still show a trading profit. Better to close down with dignity than try to continue trading against the odds and end up in Bankruptcy Court. That way, something could be salvaged from the wreckage.

Rates, too, had rocketed to heights attainable only by stores in the top trading bracket who operated from the safe base of a freehold on which the mortgage had been paid off with, preferably, no overdrafts or borrowings.

Market factors — the very things which had brought the great stores into being — were now responsible for their downfall. Such failures could be understood and forgiven, for they depended on outside forces. The rot had not come from within.

But Bonnard's had escaped even that — or thought they had.

The Bonnard family had sat back and watched with sober disapproval, if not dismay, as interior scandals had shaken other great mercantile families:

Gordon Selfridge, blossoming into a Stage Door Johnny late in life and notorious for returning to his store after hours with his current mistress. Together they had rampaged through the store like a couple of children while he had cheerfully pillaged his stock, to the delight of the lady and the dismay of the staff who were faced with unexplained shortages when they opened their departments the next morning.

William Whiteley, murdered in his own office in his Bayswater store. Shot by a young man who claimed to be his illegitimate son, never acknowledged, and taking the most terrible revenge of all: parricide.

True, the stores themselves had survived the scandals. The public demands the best merchandise available and at the lowest price; so long as that is provided, it is not disposed to worry unduly about the behind-the-scenes lives of the store management. Perhaps it was not surprising that, apart from the popular Press, the only people to note and remember such scandals were the other merchants.

Complacency again. The Bonnards had sat back in complacency, if not in judgement, watching the mistakes of others. *Oh Lord, I thank Thee that I am not as one of these.*

But now it seemed that the Bonnard's turn had come. Scandal was lurking outside, waiting to pounce. Lucien had felt its cold breath as his daughter entered the Boardroom; the formless fear had not diminished during the intervening hours. He gave a premonitory shiver and found that he could not stop shivering.

Where had it all gone wrong?

The click of the latch alerted him and he forced himself upright in his chair, lifting his head high.

'Here we are!' Maggie, too bright, too smiling—*what was he doing to her?*—hesitated in the doorway, holding the tray before her like a placatory offering. He was glad to see that she had not overloaded the plate. He did not think he would be able to eat anything at all.

'Lucien—' she crossed and set the tray before him—'I've been thinking. Do you want to stay here tonight instead of going home? It's all right with me if you do. I mean . . .' she hesitated again. 'I mean, even if you want to stay here alone. It will be all right.'

'No.' He caught her hand and pulled her close to him. 'We'll go home together tonight and come in together in the car in the morning.' He smiled wryly. 'Business as usual.'

She relaxed against him and he felt her mute gratitude that, whatever was going to happen, they would face it together.

CHAPTER 18

'I think—' Zoltan shifted uncomfortably on his camp bed as though he were becoming belatedly aware of just how inadequate it really was. 'I think that this is going to be the longest night of all.'

'Well, dear,' Dorrie said, 'it usually is. Up to now, we've had all the time in the world, but now it's like the night before Christmas with all the kiddies waiting for Father Christmas to come. That was always the longest night in the year, remember?'

'Indeed.' Zoltan did not sound comforted. 'I remember waking every few minutes and thinking I would never sleep again and that morning would never come. You mean this happens to everyone the night before the Sale begins?'

'Well, it's more likely than not. You're all keyed up, you see. Thinking about the morning, waiting for the doors to open, planning which way you'll run to get there first—'

Dorrie broke off guiltily and glanced around. Lucy Bone was huddled together with Sakim, they seemed to be communicating mainly through long meaningful looks interspersed with an occasional word; they were wrapped up in their cryptic conversation, paying no attention to anything going on around them. Not that there was all that much going on. The preliminary packing had been done shortly after they all got back from the party and the little home comforts that had sustained them during their days in the queue were now packed away into carrier bags and holdalls, with Thermos flasks on top ready to be opened for the last time in the morning to accompany a hasty breakfast.

The queue had lengthened beyond recognition as late bargain-hunters arrived for the final all-night vigil. They would be arriving all through the night, Dorrie knew from past experience, with a last-minute flurry in the morning as the early commuter trains arrived at their London termini and discharged their passengers.

'There are too many strangers here now.' Zoltan followed her gaze, catching her mood. 'They add to the restlessness.' He sighed peevishly. 'Surely one should be allowed a peaceful and uninterrupted night when tomorrow will be such a hectic day.'

'You'd think so, wouldn't you?' Dorrie found herself warming to him. Now that they were so close to parting and going their separate ways, she discovered in herself a certain fondness for them all. Perhaps it hadn't been such a bad queue, after all. It was just that it had seemed full of strangers because those near her had been so foreign. Now that a gaggle of new strangers had arrived, the familiar strangers were beginning to seem like old friends. Well, almost like old friends. There were times when even old enemies seemed more soothing company than noisy, possibly intrusive, unknown quantities.

Faye and Tim were already zipped up in their sleeping-bags, if not actually asleep then giving a determined imitation of it. They had obviously packed their mental bags as well and considered themselves as good as back in their house with their new living-room suite about to be delivered. Since they were first in the queue, they were entitled to such confidence. No one could get ahead of them.

Dorrie glanced again at Lucy Bone. If only she'd turn away from Sakim, there might be time to have a quiet word with her.

If only Zoltan weren't so wakeful. He was openly watching the rest of the queue, ears straining shamelessly for any scraps of conversation he could overhear.

Tony Adair was talking quietly with the two women behind him, although Dorrie noticed that he kept glancing towards Lucy Bone. It told her that he wasn't going to waste much time sleeping tonight. It might be his last chance to make his mark with Lucy—*he* wouldn't be looking forward to the parting of the ways in the morning. He knew that, once those ways were parted, Sakim would take good care to ensure that they stayed parted.

Sakim. It was no good, she just didn't like that one, and no mistake about it. How a nice girl had ever got herself mixed up with the likes of that . . .

But there, it went on all the time, always had. If she could have had a fifty-pence piece for all the silly girls she'd known in her lifetime who'd got entangled with the wrong man, she'd be rich. Not to mention the ones she'd read about in the papers or heard about from her friends.

The point was, most of them had come to their senses in time and straightened themselves out. Why did she have the uneasy feeling that Lucy Bone had got herself in deeper than she knew?

It crossed her mind that these few hours were also *her* last chance to try to talk to the girl—and that presented problems. She could not discuss Sakim when he was right there on the other side of Lucy Bone. Nor could she mention mink and the secret short cut to the Fur Department while Zoltan was wide awake and ready to join in any conversation right next to herself.

That left the St Edmund's, but that involved an even more delicate problem. Dorrie did not want company on her nightly foray to the Powder Room tonight. She had a private task to carry out and she did not want an observer . . . a witness.

In fact, with Faye ostensibly asleep and Lucy Bone still deep in conversation, this might be the best time to go across. Now, before the latest-comers to the queue caught on to the fact that it was the done thing for everyone to

take advantage of the St Edmund's reluctant hospi-
tality—so much more luxurious than the public con-
venience several blocks away.

With a cautious eye to see that she was not observed,
Dorrie began gathering her things together. Aware of
Zoltan's gaze, she rearranged the innocent Thermos flask
and hot-water bottle on top of her sponge-bag in the little
holdall. She had concealed the half-bottle of cherry brandy
and the small medicine bottle at the bottom of the holdall
some time ago when no one had been watching.

'You have learned how to make yourself comfortable,'
Zoltan said approvingly. 'Next time, I shall bring a hot-
water bottle—or perhaps two.' He lifted his gaze and
brooded into the distance. 'I should have thought of it
before.'

'You live and learn,' Dorrie said cheeringly. 'If it's your
first time in a queue, you did well to bring blankets and
your camp bed. Not everyone thinks of that.'

'I should not have bothered with the camp bed,' he
said. 'You did not.'

'Well,' Dorrie said, 'it *is* a little awkward to take apart
in the morning and then you have to carry it with you
while you're going round the Sale to get what you want.
It's an encumbrance, really. Although—' she added
hastily—'I'm sure it's worth it because you've been comfortable.'

'Next time—' he nodded as though a private suspicion
had been confirmed—'next time I do not bother with the
camp bed. I bring a sleeping-bag.' He looked beyond her
and added with supercilious contempt. 'At least I was not
stupid enough to bring nothing but a camp stool.'

'That's right,' Dorrie said, hoping that the sinking of
her heart didn't show in her face. If he was planning to
make a habit of queuing for Sales, it meant she might
bump into him again at some time in the future. And
that was the last thing she wanted. Especially if . . .

Dorrie stood up abruptly, inadvertently drawing the attention of the entire queue by the movement. She froze, then stooped and began smoothing out her mat and sleeping-bag as though that had been the reason for her moving. She took her time over it, and gradually the unwanted attention drifted away as people refocused on themselves and their own discomforts.

Nervously feeling that she was wasting too much time, Dorrie gave a final pat to her sleeping-bag and looked around again. She was unobserved. Tony Adair was still chatting up his sleepy neighbours. Beyond them, the newcomers were restless but completely self-absorbed. Even Zoltan had closed his eyes and fallen into a fretful doze.

Lucy Bone and Sakim rose as one, evidently having reached a point in their deliberations where more words were needed, and walked off together in search of more privacy than the queue could afford. Dorrie watched with relief as they turned the corner; that did away with the possibility that Lucy Bone might suddenly materialize in the Powder Room at an awkward moment.

The coast was as clear as it was ever going to be. Dorrie gathered up her holdall and crept quietly across the street.

A curious sense of disruption hung over the St Edmund's. The night porter gave Dorrie a harassed, almost hostile look as she passed him. It was normally beneath his dignity to notice her at all; if he did, he usually managed a polite nod, as though she were one of the guests.

'You'll be glad when it's all over.' Dorrie offered him an apologetic smile. 'Tomorrow will see the end of it.'

'Will it?' His face was grim. 'I'd like to think so.' He tilted his head infinitesimally and Dorrie realized that they were talking about two different things. He wasn't worried about the queue at all; his problem was a lot closer to home.

There were raised voices coming from the direction of the Reception Desk at the far end of the lobby. Shouting. That sort of thing just wasn't done at the St Edmund's. Except that it was being done now. No wonder the porter was upset.

'Oh dear!' Dorrie commiserated. 'Having trouble, are you?' She inclined her own head, the better to listen. There was something very familiar about the raised voice. She felt as though she could almost put a name to it — but not quite. Perhaps because it did not usually deliver lines in such an unpleasant tone.

The porter shook his head gloomily. 'We don't have the class of people we used to have in this hotel,' he said. 'Not like the old days . . .'

'Not at all . . .' Dorrie agreed, edging away from him, moving towards the main lobby, ignoring the staircase down to the Powder Room. There was no great hurry about that and her curiosity had been aroused.

'Please, sir, if you'll just step into my office —' The man gestured towards the Manager's Office tucked away behind the Reception Desk.

'No way!' The familiar voice trumpeted. 'You're not going to sweep *me* under the carpet like a pile of dirt.'

'I assure you, sir . . .'

'Yeah, sure, you assure. You've been saying that all along. I don't want your assurance — I want my rights!'

'May I point out to you —' The night manager's voice chilled, although it was still fairly clear that he wished the day manager were there behind him and perhaps the rest of the office staff as well.

'May I point out that you arrived without a reservation. When we accepted you, we made it clear that you could have the Penthouse suite you requested for only —'

'No, you may not!' Brick Ronson thundered. Unlike the night manager, with only an uneasy desk clerk behind him, Brick was backed up by Belva Barrie, a nervous looking man who was probably a minor minion of the Production Unit, and two rather sinister, very heavy men who might have been personal bodyguards.

'We explicitly stated—' The night manager stuck to his guns. 'We explained that the Penthouse Suite was available only until Sheikh Mohammad al—'

'Shake yourself!' Brick Ronson snarled. 'I'm in the Penthouse Suite and I'm staying there! Possession,' he added, with an air of conscious virtue at being able to pull such a quote out of the hat, 'is nine points of the law!'

'Eleven,' Belva Barrie said automatically. It was the first time her voice had been added to the scene. She did not seem particularly upset at the prospect of moving; she was more concerned to have the quotation correct.

'Nevertheless,' the night manager said, 'the agreement was that you would vacate the Penthouse Suite when the Sheikh arrived and he is due the first thing in the morning. That means that we would like you to—'

'I'm not moving!'

'Brick,' Belva said, 'they *did* tell us that when we checked in and we *did* promise to move when they wanted the penthouse.'

'So now I've changed my mind. I like it in the penthouse, I'm all settled there. I don't want to have to pack again. Let the Sheikh take your other suite and stay in it until *I'm* ready to leave. Then *he* can move into the penthouse—if he thinks it's worth the bother.'

'Madam,' the night manager appealed to his new and unexpected ally, '*you* remember our original agreement—'

'You keep out of this!' Brick snapped at her. 'And don't you try to drag her into it!' He turned back to the night manager without having noticed the flare of anger in her eyes.

'It *was* an agreement.' The night manager tried to be

both firm and conciliating. 'I'm afraid the St Edmund's must insist that you honour it. We will disturb you as little as possible—the housekeeper will personally take care of your packing. Meanwhile, if you would all like to be my guests in the St Edmund's Bar, we can arrange the transfer as smoothly and quickly as possible.'

In his agitation the night manager threw out his arm in a sweeping gesture, including Dorrie in the entourage invited as his guests. Only Belva Barrie noticed and she gave Dorrie a friendly wink and a nod which plain as day acknowledged the joke and drew her into the charmed circle. Enchanted, Dorrie edged closer.

'After all—' Rashly, the night manager tried to consolidate the ground he imagined he had gained. 'Had the Sheikh already been in residence when you arrived, you would have gone into the alternative accommodation in the first place. And I'm sure you would have found it eminently satisfactory—'

'Alternative accommodation,' Brick mocked, 'Alternative accommodation. Just what *is* this alternative accommodation you keep talking about?'

'One of our most sought-after suites,' the night manager assured him. 'Only two floors below the penthouse and just as luxurious in every way. It also has its own private lift and is usually fully booked. Although,' he added hastily, 'we have several other highly desirable suites. But, by great good fortune, this *is* one of the best and you can move in immediately. The Bridal Suite.'

'*What?*' Brick's face shaded from pink to dark red and Dorrie realized how he had come by his name. He thrust his darkened face into the night manager's and demanded, 'Are you trying to be sarcastic?'

'Brick, please—' Belva tugged at his arm.

'I assure you, sir—'

'Think you're funny, do you?' Behind Brick, the two bodyguards moved up on either side, flexing their muscles.

'Brick, *stop!*'

He shook her off, but seemed to regain some control over his temper. 'All right.' He drew himself up. 'Now get this straight: I am in the Penthouse Suite and I am staying there. If you let your housekeeper, your maids, your porters, or anyone else, lay one finger on any one of my things, you are going to find yourself in the God-damnedest legal hassle you ever saw. It won't do you or your precious hotel any good, no matter who wins. Furthermore —'

'I think you're being unreasonable, Brick,' Belva said quietly.

'Who asked you?'

'You're making a mountain out of a molehill —'

'*I'm* not, no. That's what this fellow here is doing —' He gestured towards the night manager. 'Turning out a perfectly good guest — who was here first — for the sake of a — a —'

'Brick,' she said warningly.

'Maybe the dollar isn't what it used to be.' Brick returned his attack to the night manager — 'but you'd better remember that the oil is running out. When they've got nothing left but dry wells and camels, there'll still be plenty of dollars and they'll be better than any other legal tender because they'll still be backed by Yankee ingenuity and know-how. That'll make them twice as good as any other currency and you'd better believe it! We've still got the top scientists and technicians and they'll pull some aces out of their sleeves that will have the rest of the world blinking —'

'*Brick!*'

'All right, that's all I've got to say. Except that we're going back upstairs now and staying there. I'm hanging out the "Do not disturb" sign and I want you to make sure I'm *not* disturbed. I don't want any more aggravation — I just want a quiet night.' He stepped back, leaving the night manager speechless and on the verge of wringing his hands.

You could see everybody's point of view, Dorrie decided. There was the poor night manager, caught between an important Middle-Eastern potentate and an important Hollywood star. No matter what he did, there were going to be hurt feelings, insulted VIPs and, quite probably, repercussions.

On the other hand, it *was* a bit of cheek to tell important people like Brick Ronson and Belva Barrie that they were only to be allowed the best accommodation on sufferance — until somebody more important came along and wanted it and then they'd have to clear out. You couldn't blame Brick Ronson for being highly annoyed.

Although it seemed that Belva could blame him. He was half way across the lobby before he realized that she wasn't with him and turned back to find her murmuring apologies to the night manager.

'Come on,' he said. 'We've wasted enough time down here. We've got an early call in the morning.'

'No,' Belva said. 'It isn't fair, Brick. We promised we'd give up the suite —'

'To hell with that!' He snatched at her arm. 'Let's get some sleep.'

'No, not in the Penthouse Suite. It isn't ours.' She stepped back and bumped into Dorrie. Impulsively she linked arms with her. 'I'd sleep in that queue across the street first!'

She meant it, too, you could tell that. She smiled challengingly at them all and backed away from Brick, pulling Dorrie with her.

'Let's go,' she said. 'You'll make room for me in the queue, won't you?'

Dorrie smiled back in a moment of delicious complicity before the realization of her plight swamped her with cold horror.

How could she do what she had to do with Belva Barrie in tow?

CHAPTER 19

It was more than an hour later that Dorrie got back to her place in the queue. Alone, thank heavens. To her great relief, Belva and Brick had eventually made it up and were now supervising the removal of their belongings to the lesser suite.

'Hah! We were getting worried about you,' Zoltan greeted her. 'We wondered if you were unwell. We were about to send someone over to see if you were all right.'

Just as well they hadn't. Ten minutes ago she had been in the Powder Room carefully transferring the contents of the medicine bottle into the half-bottle of cherry brandy. Just suppose someone had walked in on that! Dorrie felt quite giddy at the thought of her close escape.

'I'm fine,' she said quickly. 'I've been talking to those nice film people. They insisted I join them for a drink. I never thought I'd be worrying anyone. I'm sorry.'

'You make friends everywhere, I think,' Zoltan sighed. 'I wish I could learn the secret from you. People do not like me easily.' He sighed again. 'Sometimes I think I am not even an acquired taste.'

'Oh, you mustn't think that,' Dorrie said ambiguously. She was beginning to feel sorry for him and with it came a pang of guilt for what she was going to do. Not enough guilt to stop her, she decided, but enough to make her uncomfortable.

She looked quickly at Lucy Bone, huddled in her sleeping-bag now, but still awake, staring bleakly into the night, and her resolve strengthened again. The poor child deserved a break after hanging on in the queue for so long, even after she had learned that there was no real hope of getting what she wanted.

Or, an uneasy thought came to Dorrie, *had the girl remained in the queue because her boy-friend had forced her to? Sure of getting what he wanted, too jealous to allow her to leave. Was he keeping her here so that he could watch her and make sure she wasn't off meeting another, perhaps nicer, man?*

Which wouldn't be hard. Although she had begun by disliking him, Dorrie was now beginning to think that even Zoltan was nicer than Sakim.

'I shall go across to the St Edmund's now.' Zoltan stood up. 'But you will see,' he added gloomily. 'I will return straightaway. No one will take to *me* and invite *me* to stay and have a drink with them.'

Dorrie almost wished she could do something about it. She watched until he was safely inside the entrance, then turned to Lucy Bone.

'Don't say anything, dear—' She kept her voice low. 'Just listen and let me tell you. We've got to be quick before he comes back. Now, in the morning—'

'Morning?' Lucy Bone popped up on one elbow, like a jack-in-the-box, looking strangely alarmed. 'What about the morning?'

Behind her, Sakim edged forward, his eyes alert and hostile.

'When the doors open, you be ready to follow along right behind me. No matter what happens, don't let it delay you.'

'Happens?' Lucy Bone's voice rose. Sakim's hand moved towards the foot of her sleeping-bag. Dorrie was too intent on giving instructions to notice.

'If you can get to the Fur Department first, the coat is yours. After all,' she justified, 'you were here nearly as long as he was, and you've been waiting all this time—'

'That coat!' Lucy Bone fell back, slapping Sakim's hand away. 'It doesn't matter,' she said listlessly. 'I don't care any more.'

'It's too early to lose hope,' Dorrie said, giving as much encouragement as she could without getting near the truth. 'I'll show you—there's a short cut to the Fur Department. You're younger than he is. You can run faster and—'

Lucy Bone gave a short harsh laugh. 'I'm sorry,' she apologized immediately, seeing the effect it had on Dorrie. 'It's very kind of you to bother, but—'

'No bother at all,' Dorrie lied cheerfully. May Lucy Bone never discover just how much bother it had been! 'It's on my way. You just come along with me to my turning and I'll point you in the right direction.'

'Mad!' Sakim muttered it to Lucy, but Dorrie heard him. 'All the English are mad!'

She wouldn't lower herself to bandy words with a creature like that! Dorrie compressed her lips and sat back. And there was Zoltan, returning already. There would be no chance to say anything more. It was all very unsatisfactory.

Dorrie tried to settle herself for some rest, but knew that she was too keyed-up. It was a pity that she had nothing left to read. She closed her eyes and sighed. It was going to be a long night.

It was a long night. Maggie huddled under the bedclothes and tried to pretend that she was still asleep. Lucien was pacing the floor again with a heavy monotonous tread. There was no point in letting him see that he had awakened her; there was nothing left to say. They had already covered every angle and come to no satisfactory conclusions.

He was at the window now. If he opened it again . . . She ground her teeth and forced herself to remain silent. After a few moments, the pacing resumed.

Poor Lucien. This must be one of the longest nights of his life.

Come to think of it, she had known shorter ones herself. *Damn Lucinda, anyway!*

Damn Lucinda . . . damn Lucinda . . . Repeating the comforting litany, Maggie drifted off into a light doze, still conscious of the unending footsteps.

Lucien Bonnard paced on through the night.

Foster kept watch from the window at the half-landing of the staircase. When he saw the limousine turn the corner, he would descend the stairs and be waiting at the front entrance as the limousine drew to a halt in front of the store.

Lucien Bonnard would descend from the limousine and pause to shake hands with the first half-dozen people in the queue and wish them success. Then he would approach the entrance. Foster would swing back the doors and the Sales hordes would pour through in Lucien Bonnard's wake.

It was a ceremonial Foster always enjoyed, but this morning he was increasingly uneasy. He wished the day were safely over.

Lucinda Bonnard was one of the first half-dozen people in *this* year's queue.

Now it was all a question of timing. Dorrie stole a worried glance at her watch. Half past eight and the doors would open at nine. When ought she to offer Zoltan his stirrup cup? How long before the secret ingredient took effect? Would it work properly?

In its undiluted form the effect was almost instantaneous. But there had been quite a bit of cherry brandy left in the half-bottle, even after she had poured off enough into her Thermos of tea to make room for the contents of the medicine bottle. And another worry: was it mixed properly, or would it all sink to the bottom and be useless?

Surreptitiously, Dorrie reached into her holdall and tried to shake the bottle without attracting attention.

And then, didn't the size and weight of the victim — She pulled her mind back in horror. *No, no, the person drinking* — Didn't that have something to do with the length of time it would take to work on him? If the effect were delayed too long, he could have already reached the Fur Department and bought the coat before he was stricken. On the other hand, if she gave it to him too soon, he might have it over and done with before the doors opened and be back in the queue in time to rush in with the rest of them.

She wished she had paid more attention to that nice book on the Borgias the librarian had recommended recently.

All around her, the long-term members of the queue were making their preparations for departure. Sleeping-bags were rolled into the smallest possible parcel and stowed away in carrier bags, several trips had been made to the nearest litter bin to dispose of rubbish and jettison unwanted oddments which might impede progress when the doors opened.

She would have to give a thought herself as to where to get rid of the evidence once she was out of sight. Not in the store, nor anyplace where it might be connected with her. Any remaining contents of the half-bottle would have to be poured down a drain somewhere, lest some innocent come across it and risk drinking it. She didn't mind Zoltan, but she'd hate to have some poor meths drinker on her conscience. Perhaps it would be safer to break the bottle and throw the pieces into a litter bin in some public place, perhaps a railway station. She would decide later; the bottle would be safe enough in her holdall while she bought the fridge-freezer and — oh yes — the pair of roller-skates for Young Ron.

Ahead of her, Zoltan was still struggling to dismantle

his camp bed. She wondered if he had had as much trouble putting it up. It seemed to be an old and excessively complicated contraption; possibly he had brought it with him from his native land. It didn't look English.

'I have learned—' He caught her watching him and shook his head ruefully. 'Not again do I bother with such foolishness. Next time, I will have a sleeping-bag like the rest of you.'

'You *do* seem to be having a time with it.' Dorrie hoped she sounded sufficiently sympathetic. Enough to make her next remark seem natural.

'Why don't you have a—' Her voice broke and she tried again, lifting the half-bottle of cherry brandy out of her holdall. 'Why don't you have a stirrup cup with me before we're off on our hunt?'

'Ah—ha!' He won the battle and flourished the last metal rod at her as the canvas collapsed on the pavement. 'To celebrate, perhaps I shall! It is most kind of you.'

'Not at all.' Dorrie turned her face away guiltily as she gave the bottle a final swirl and half-filled the generous plastic cup.

'But what is this? Do you not drink too?' He frowned as he accepted the cup.

'Oh, I have mine here. It's a bit too powerful for me as it is, so I've mixed it with my tea.' Dorrie uncapped her Thermos flask. 'I thought you'd rather have it strong, but of course if you'd prefer—' She offered the Thermos, holding her breath.

'No, no.' He waved it away. 'You are quite right. I would rather have it strong.' He sniffed at it and appeared about to sip.

'Of course,' Dorrie babbled anxiously, 'If it were a real stirrup cup, it wouldn't have a base to it, so that you'd drink it all down at one swallow. It was handed up to the huntsmen after they'd mounted, you see, so they'd no place to put it down anyway. They simply drained the cup and handed it back to their grooms.'

'Then I must do the same.' He beamed at her. 'Even though I have no horse and no groom.'

As she had hoped, he tossed back his head and gulped it down. That was the rather endearing thing about foreigners: they were so anxious to conform that they could be persuaded to do almost anything if they thought it was part of the English way of life.

'Yes.' He coughed and handed the cup back to her. 'It is indeed powerful. I am not surprised you wished to weaken it. For a woman, it is more suitable that way.'

'Would you like another tot?' Dorrie offered.

'Er . . . I think not, at the moment.' He swallowed again and forced a smile. 'I must finish packing up my things.'

Dorrie sipped at her heavily-laced tea, wishing that she could avoid doing so. She had a suspicion that the combination of tea and cherry brandy would taste foul at any time and it was certainly not the drink for first thing in the morning. Under Zoltan's watchful eye, however, she had to continue.

On the other side of Lucy Bone, Sakim appeared to be twitching with excitement. She hoped it was excitement; but it must be. She'd have noticed if he'd been smoking anything—although not necessarily if he'd swallowed anything. How that poor misguided child had ever taken up with someone like that . . .

Even as she watched, Sakim tried to help Lucy Bone fold up her sleeping-bag, tearing at it as he did so. It came out of Lucy's grasp and she nearly dropped it.

With a cry of rage, Sakim slapped her across the face.

It brought a gasp of concern from the others in the queue and it brought Tony Adair to his feet ready to fight.

'No, please—' Lucy tried to stop him. 'It's all right. Sakim didn't hurt me. He's just over-excited. Please—

don't start anything.'

'*He* started it.' But Tony Adair backed away, baffled at her air of muted hysteria.

'It's all right.' Dorrie came forward quickly, knowing what she had to do. 'I'll take care of this.'

Tony Adair gave her an odd look, but seemed prepared to let her handle it. Absently he reached into his pocket and brought out a small camera. He stood there toying with it, as though he had lost all interest in the proceedings, but Dorrie could sense that he was still watchful.

'Now, then,' Dorrie said to Sakim in soothing tones. 'Of course you're over-excited with the big Sale about to start and it being your very first one. What you need is a nice little drink —'

Under Sakim's bemused gaze, she poured the remaining cherry brandy into a cup until it nearly overflowed.

'You just drink this right down —' She handed it to him. 'It's just what you need. It will do you a world of good.'

Sakim seemed of the same opinion. He seized the cup as she finished pouring and drained it.

'Thank you . . .' he said hesitantly.

'Oh, that's quite all right,' Dorrie said sweetly. 'You deserved it.'

She glanced once more at her watch: it was seven minutes to nine.

CHAPTER 20

Across the street, six large burly men emerged from the St Edmund's, had a brief word with the doorman, glancing towards the queue as they did so, then four of them descended the steps and separated to walk towards opposite ends of the street.

Dorrie recognized the two who had remained in the doorway as the bodyguards with the film people. The other four, although they were swarthy and looked as though they might be more comfortable in a burnoose, were obviously of the same ilk.

They had just reached their stations at the ends of the street when a sleek grey limousine turned the corner. At the same moment, another limousine entered the street from the other end and rolled towards Bonnard's and the St Edmund's.

Dorrie watched comfortably as the cars approached. One was probably coming to collect the film people — nine o'clock would undoubtedly be what they considered an 'early call'. The other must contain Mr Bonnard himself, coming to open his splendid Gala Centenary Sale.

But no, she corrected her first assumption on seeing a colourful flag fluttering from a mast on the radiator cap, the grey limousine could not be for the film people, it looked too official. It must be the Sheikh arriving to take possession of his Penthouse Suite.

The queue rustled expectantly. Dorrie tried to concentrate on the limousines, but could not resist a sideways glance. Sakim's forehead was besprinkled with perspiration and he kept swallowing convulsively. Zoltan seemed in better state, but he was beginning to wear a worried expression.

The first limousine was drawing up in front of the St Edmund's now. The doorman hurried down the steps to open the nearside door.

'*Hiaa-yiaa—*!' Shouting something incomprehensible, Sakim dived into the middle of the street and dropped to one knee, levelling a gun with both hands as the Sheikh emerged from the limousine.

But the shot went wild as the first spasm of retching caught and shook him.

'Excuse me—' Almost simultaneously, Zoltan clutched at his stomach and darted from the queue, aiming for the sanctuary and decent privacy of the Men's Room in the St Edmund's, heedless of anything between him and his goal.

Sakim struggled for control and raised the gun again for a second shot. Zoltan collided with him, sending him flying and falling himself. For a moment, entangled, they fought to get up, then, overcome by misery, fell back retching and violently sick.

The bodyguards converged on them from both ends of the street.

Cats eat grass when they feel the need to empty their stomachs. The emetic favoured by Dorrie's mother had been a nasty but unforgettable Victorian concoction called Syrup of Ipecac. The results were the same and equally unpleasant.

Dorrie averted her eyes in time to see Lucy Bone start forward. She caught at Lucy's skirt and pulled her off-balance. Lucy fell to the pavement, struggling.

'Please,' she said. 'I'm supposed to help if—'

Dorrie wasn't quite sure what was going on, but she knew enough not to let that little madam plunge out into the mess in the middle of the street and ruin the rest of her life. She hung on grimly as the girl battled to rise and free herself.

'Let me go!' Lucy struggled desperately, almost sobbing. How had it all gone so wrong? The Sheikh should be lying dead in the gutter now — a tyrant destroyed. She and Sakim should have escaped in the confusion — rushing around the corner and utilizing the key she wore round her neck to slip through the staff entrance, thus inextricably embroiling Bonnard's in the scandal. It would ruin their Middle-Eastern business and perhaps even bring down the store itself — to the destruction of another tyrant.

If she could get free, dash out into the street and seize the gun from Sakim, she might still be able to —

'Keep still! You don't know what you're doing!' Lucy was back on her feet and Dorrie found herself in hand-to-hand combat she was ill-equipped for. She looked to Tony Adair for help, but he had his camera to his eye and was busily recording the scenes being played out in the centre of the street. Anything less dramatic was of no interest to him.

'Let me go!' Slippery as an eel, the girl nearly twisted out of her hands.

There was nothing else for it! Dorrie kicked the girl's ankles out from under her and as she fell, sat down heavily on top of her.

There was a whoosh of air from Lucy's lungs and she abruptly lost interest in the proceedings.

Then help was upon them. The front door opened and Foster darted out to lift Dorrie to her feet and pick up the semi-conscious girl. The second limousine had stopped farther up the street when the firing started and now Mr Bonnard and his lady-friend were running towards them.

Out in the street, the bodyguards had taken harsh command of the situation, although there sounded the reassuring klaxon of an approaching police car in the distance.

Thankfully Dorrie relinquished her last hold on the girl as the people from Bonnard's surrounded them. She watched as they spirited the girl through the entrance and disappeared into the store with her, leaving Dorrie with a new and puzzling question:

Had Lucy Bone actually sobbed out 'Daddy' as Mr Bonnard bore her away?

For all that Bonnard's had been a bit late in opening, due to all the commotion outside, everything had gone quite well. The fridge-freezer was safely acquired for George and Sandra, with the promise of delivery within the week. The roller-skates for Young Ron were in her carrier bag and Dorrie now felt free to roam about the store to see how the others from the queue were doing.

She found Faye and Tim still in the Furniture Department, beaming with triumph and earnestly debating whether or not to buy a corner cabinet with some of the money they had saved on their bargain suite. Dorrie cast her vote in favour before moving on.

She didn't look for Tony Adair. He had sprinted past her when the doors opened, calling out that he was going to get his film equipment and then rush down to Fleet Street to sell the pictures he had just taken. Dorrie rather thought that the police might like to look at them first, but he hadn't waited for her opinion and doubtless he would find out soon enough what the police views were on his behaviour. Personally she didn't blame him. He ought to get a tidy little sum for pictures as exciting as those and it was nice to see a pleasant young man get on in the world.

She was trying not to think about an equally ambitious but less pleasant young man when a hand fell on her shoulder.

'There you are!' Maggie beamed. 'We've been looking for you — we hoped you hadn't left the store yet. Lucien wants to see you. Come along —'

'Ooo-er, yes, certainly.' Guiltily conscious of the bottle

with dregs of drugged brandy in her holdall, Dorrie
followed her to the private lift. Maggie pushed the button
for the executive floor, still beaming and burbling.

'You must know how wonderful you've been,' Maggie
said. '*We* know—and Lucien wants to do something for
you. You won't be silly or stuffy about it, will you? You'll
let him?'

'Why, er . . .' Dorrie tightened her grip on her holdall.
Suppose she should drop it at this stage, the bottle break,
and the rich betraying smell of cherry brandy call attention to rather more than the Bonnard's people had in
mind?

Lucien Bonnard himself came forward to meet her,
taking her hastily-freed hand in both his. Now she had
both carrier bag and holdall in one hand, her nervousness
increased. For a moment, she thought he was going to kiss
her on both cheeks and had to remind herself that the
French in him was several generations back, despite his
name. He was as English as she was.

Behind him, she saw a familiar face . . . Lucy Bone?

'You know everyone, I believe—' He led her forward.
'Foster, Maggie . . . my daughter, Lucinda—'

No, not Lucy Bone. Dorrie had been wondering about
that for some little time now. She smiled and nodded,
betraying no surprise.

'Allow me, madam.' Foster relieved her of her bags,
depositing them gently in a corner of the room. She
began to feel slightly more at ease.

'Oh!' She saw the full-length mink draped over a chair.
'You got it then, dear!' she said triumphantly, before
abruptly recollecting. Lucinda Bonnard had had no need
to queue for anything in the store. 'No, of course not. You
never really wanted it.' *Lucy Bone* had been no more
interested in the mink than Sakim had cared about a Persian carpet for his mother. At least she'd guessed right
about *that*.

'We removed it from the Sale,' Lucien Bonnard said. 'Mr Zoltan will be joining us shortly. It seems appropriate that he have it. He was first in the queue for it, after all.'

'Only fair,' Dorrie agreed, blushing for her own gullibility. She'd been a mug and no mistake. Worse. But with any luck she might get out of here before Zoltan appeared to claim his prize—

The door behind her opened again and a sinking feeling deep within her told her who had just come in.

'We are all here, I see.' Zoltan's voice contrived to be both weak and arrogant. 'Those of us who deserve to be,' he amended.

Dorrie continued walking until she reached Lucy's— Lucinda's—side. Lucinda gave her a pale smile of welcome, looking drowsy. They'd given her something to calm her down, no doubt.

'Feeling better, are you, dear?' Dorrie was flooded with relief. You never could tell, the girl might still have been in a fury, blaming her for the ruination of a careful plan.

'She'll be better soon.' Maggie moved protectively to Lucinda's side. 'The doctor has just left to arrange everything. She's going straight to a nursing home for a nice long rest.'

Where the police can't get at her, no matter what Sakim confesses. Barricaded safely behind wealth and privilege—and why not? Although Lucinda had been intent upon murder and scandal, she'd have thought differently if they had actually happened. It would have been too nasty. Not the sort of thing a nice English girl should get up to—especially one with Lucinda Bonnard's background. Not that that stopped them these days.

'She'll come to her senses, you mean.' Tony Adair had come in with Zoltan. 'That was a prize piece of stupidity,' he snapped at the girl. 'You nearly got yourself set up for a good long stretch!'

'I know,' she agreed meekly, yawning. 'I'm just beginning to realize . . . '

'It will all seem a bad dream soon,' Dorrie said comfortingly. It often happened like this. Once they'd discovered
how close to the wind they'd actually been sailing, reaction set in. A nursing home was the best place for
Lucinda while she sorted herself out. With Tony Adair
standing by, it might happen more quickly than they
expected.

'Everything has ended well,' Zoltan said, with magnifi-
cent self-assurance. 'Thanks to me.'

'That's right.' Tony Adair fluttered an eyelid at Dorrie.
'It was damned brave of you — rushing out into the street
like that, without a thought for your own safety. You
probably saved the Sheikh's life.'

'That is what he has told me.' Zoltan was stroking the
mink complacently, evidently going to forgive them for
not having saved the silver fox as well. 'He took me to his
suite and insisted that I have one of his suits — ' He preened
before them in his new finery. 'To replace my own, so unfortunately ruined. He is most grateful.'

'So he ought to be,' Dorrie said faintly. 'And you not
well and all. I do hope you're feeling better.'

For a moment she thought she had gone too far. Zoltan
rasied his head and gave her an enigmatic look.

'I shall be fine soon,' he said. 'The Sheikh was most
sympathetic that the excitement should have affected me
so. His wife wishes the mink coat at great profit to me.
Furthermore, the Sheikh has appointed me his Purchas-
ing Agent in the United Kingdom and Europe. I believe I
am on my way to making my fortune. For that, one can
forgive much discomfort.'

'Splendid!' Lucien Bonnard turned to Dorrie, extend-
ing a white envelope embossed with the gold Bonnard's
seal. 'And Mrs Witson is on her way to visit her friends in
America. Just present the voucher at the Travel Department and they'll arrange everything for you. I'd suggest

you fly one way and return by the *Queen Elizabeth 2* — first class, of course. Oh, and Maggie will help you choose presents from Bonnard's to take to your friends. With Bonnard's compliments.'

'Ooh!' No doubt she'd think of something to say later, but Dorrie was momentarily speechless.

'And now let us all drink to a most successful opening to Bonnard's Centenary Year. In anything you like —' There was a conspiratorial twinkle in his eyes as he glanced at Dorrie. 'Even cherry brandy, if you would prefer.'

'No, thank you,' Dorrie said faintly. 'To tell you the truth, I've gone off it somehow.'

卌 卌 卌 卌Ⅱ 3 3 44 |

46 6773 2 0001

8